DEEPER STILL
BY SARAH COLLIVER

Sequel to 'IN DEEP'

Tate is young, beautiful and successful. Her past is firmly behind her, and her eyes fixed on the future. Her shadowy past may have funded her lifestyle, but she deserved every penny, for what she suffered, right?

Ellie is determined to get her hands on everything her dad, Bill, had stolen from him whilst he perished in the fire. It is rightfully hers after all. But she is plagued by demons, and her drug habit feeds her darkness. Her arrival will shake Tate's new life to the core.

This story will sweep you up into the eye of a storm, as you watch the events unfold from both perspectives.
Will anyone survive, as they fall DEEPER STILL?

TATE

It was 1.30 am and the Spanish air was still unbearably hot. Tate shifted onto her back and sighed; her rustic town house lacked air-conditioning. She relied on a breeze flowing through the open window to cool her down, but the night air was heavy, and no breeze could be felt. She jumped with the scrape of the rusty bolt across her front door. He was home.

Mauricio fought to remove his tangled jeans, and loose change scattered over the tiled floor, "Shit," he laughed, and shushed himself. Tate closed her eyes tight and turned away from the footsteps staggering upstairs. He reached her bedroom door, dropped his clothes to the floor and slipped beneath the sheet. He wriggled up close and traced his finger from her neck down to the small of her back. She did not stir. Hopefully he would roll over and fall asleep; his rummy breath turned her stomach. On reaching her knickers he gently rolled them lower and rubbed her buttock in circles with the palm of his hand, "Tate wake up," he whispered in her ear and nibbled his way from her neck to her shoulder.

Tate turned onto her back and opened her eyes, "you woke me!"

"It will be worth it," although his eyes were full of drunken desire, his words were slurred.

"I'm tired," she sighed and smacked away his wandering hands.

"It won't take long…"

"Wow, what a tempting offer," she pushed him off her legs. He fell sideways and was already snoring by the time she reached the bathroom. Her mind began to replay images of Bill again. He knew what she liked, she would never have refused him anything, in fact they did things she could never repeat with anyone else, her cheeks flushed at the thought. Bill was a hard act to follow in the bedroom. He had an edge and yet was capable of being gentle, sometimes.

She should stop comparing them. That's what Irena said: 'You can't put a lion and a tabby cat side by side and expect them to behave the same.' She always tutted when Tate said anything about Bill, and she understood why, but sometimes no matter what someone does to you, part of them lingers, however hard you try to forget. She hated Bill, but the romantic fantasy she created about him back then, well that was the part she hankered for.

Mauricio was enjoying a great lifestyle at her expense, he went to 'work' every night, played gigs in bars and then came home pissed up. In the early days, she loved to watch him perform. She even got butterflies when he would sing, look her way and smile. Being serenaded was flattering, especially when there was usually a small cluster of women swooning as he sung. They would stare jealously when he would make his way through the crowds towards her for a kiss. The novelty soon wore off. Where was his depth, ambition, drive? He created those impressions in his singing, but it was a façade, only a performance. He couldn't earn a pittance playing gigs forever – surely that was more of a hobby? She flushed the toilet, washed her hands and headed for the spare room to escape the rum-induced snoring.

Since Bill, life was full of ups and downs. Initially she was on a high and felt empowered and strong on her return to the UK. But her time spent there only confirmed that her heart lay in Spain, despite what she had endured. She missed Irena and their partying too. The feeling of money in her pocket was nice, but she had no clear direction back then. It was whilst buying a bouquet for her mum's birthday, she saw an advert for a trainee florist, and without thinking about it, applied. She knew this world, having spent her youth putting flowers together, to earn money for clothes and make-up. And it seemed like the right way to go. Whilst on the course, her natural ability flourished. The Latin names were like poetry, and she was astounded with the variety and sheer volume there was to learn about.

Irena was quick to inform her when the old tobacconist next to Bazaar came up for sale and she wasted no time getting things organised for her return. It was the perfect size for a small florist, and they were able to combine forces and knock-through, to create one shop. The day she got the keys, she felt on top of the world. It was a dream to work so closely with Irena. They made a great team, a force to be reckoned with. She hadn't looked back since, and Spain now felt like home.

Mauricio was a convenient distraction; a rebound when she most needed it, but she had outgrown him, and he irritated her more every day. It was time to end whatever it was they had, but it could wait until tomorrow. The clock said 2am, she needed sleep. Irena's yoga voice crept into her head and instructed her to listen to her breathing and slow it down, rhythmically. As sleep took her, Bill arrived, she was back at his villa in the shower, and he smelt so good...

***

She chose her town house, because of the location mainly, although the clincher was the tatty blue Spanish door. It was the kind you stop and photograph, because it is so typical of the region, and she wanted one for herself. First spied in the window of the property agent, she wasted no time and arranged a viewing the following day, having dreamed of settling in a house like this. The last six months had been a joy to decorate and accessorise the rooms. Finally, her own place, with no fear of anyone taking it away.

Mauricio was still out cold, in his usual post work slumber, as she closed the door behind her and headed for the shop. A busy day lay ahead with flowers for a party to organise, as well as covering Irena's, who was visiting a stockist in Malaga. Plus, now she had the added pressure of catching Mauricio at some point, although she knew he wouldn't be surprised by her breakup chat, it was more of a formality.

With the turn of the key, her senses awoke with the scent of lilies filling the air. She smiled, grateful that this was her little empire, opened the wooden shutters and switched on her gentle jazz music. Her apprentice would arrive soon with their morning coffee, to aid her bleary eyes. She would need a constant stream of caffeine to get to lunchtime. She switched on the lights and slid down the heavy bolt on Irena's door. Lingering incense permeated the air, and a gentle

4

tingle of the wind-chimes as she flew past, rooted her to the floor and for a moment she felt like the luckiest woman in the world. Irena really had created an oasis of calm. She checked her watch, and at 8.30 precisely, a waft of coffee preceded the arrival of her apprentice, Jo. The end of her floristry course loomed, and her shoulder bag bulged with her coursework. Tate hoped she would stay on afterwards and work for her, there was enough work for two.

"Morning boss," Jo handed a steaming cup to Tate.

"If ever I needed coffee, it's today."

"But you say that every day!" Jo hung up her bag and tied on her apron.

"But today I really mean it, did you notice if the bakery had any pastries left? If so, pop over and grab us one each before we start...can't work on an empty stomach, can we?"

Jo smiled, and popped her coffee on the counter, "I'm on it, two pastries coming up."

With a grateful sigh, Tate hoped the arrival of her breakfast would silence the groans of her rumbling tummy.

ELLIE

The heavy thud of music ricocheted through her body and her bare feet navigated the throng of sweaty dancers. Hypnotic strobe lights disguised the tatty interior of the club

5

as she wove amongst the crowd touching and feeling anyone who turned her way.

It was always planned as a big night, the last for a while on the coast, before she moved up into the mountains to retrace the footsteps of her dad. Fi would leave in the morning, and she could get to work on finding the truth. The bouncers among the clubs they partied in, offered little information, except the mumbling of a rumour, that the fire which killed her dad was started on purpose. She could have figured that much out for herself. No one would give any names.

When Bill failed to appear after the fire, his solicitor dug as deep as he could into his sketchy world but came up with nothing. His 'official' bank account remained untouched, and not one sighting was ever reported. No one seemed to care too much either. Only his brother was still alive, and he had severed ties with Bill many years before, distancing himself from any chance of dodgy gangs knocking on his door. He felt the same way her mum felt – that they were all better off without him, but this just didn't sit right with Ellie and anyway, he must have loved her a little if he was prepared to give her so much money. If no one else cared, then the least she could do, was dig around and try and find out more about what happened. Besides, where had all his money gone? Someone was sitting pretty, living a good life on his hard-earned cash. That cash should have gone to her.

Fi thrust a glass into her hand, "Sex on the beach. I've been looking for you for ages, don't keep wandering off."

Ellie swiped the glass and downed the drink in one before wiping her lips with her wrist, "Hey, who's paying for this trip? I give out the orders here. Anyway, I promised you the best night, and aren't you having the best time of your life?" Ellie did not wait for an answer, as some random guy pulled her into a deep kiss. The empty glass smashed to the floor, and she pushed him back, focussed as best as she could, and liked what she saw. They dived towards a dingy corner where at first, she kissed him hungrily, but the moment passed, and she clambered off him.

"Hey, where you going?" he called.

"Don't touch what you can't afford, mate," she hissed back.

"Fucking pricktease." he shouted, as he straightened himself up.

Ellie swung around and punched him hard on the jaw, "What the fuck did you call me? Pricktease wasn't it?" She kneed him hard in the crotch and he doubled over with pain. She grabbed his hair and pulled his head back, "That's the only action your pricks getting tonight." Then she kissed his forehead and left him folded up on the floor.

"Fi, come on, let's go." Ellie staggered towards the exit.

"You're hurting me, Stop! what's the rush?"

"Full of sleazeballs, not my style..."

The hot air on the street, mixed with the festering rubbish awaiting collection, turned her stomach and she threw up along the sidewall of the club. She steadied herself with one hand on the wall and then stood up straight.

"Get a room," she threw towards the couple who were frantically screwing against the wall of the alley, "a fucking alley, that's classy." She wiped her mouth and staggered up the street towards her apartment. "Keep up will you, let's get back."

"I didn't even get the last drink I paid for..."

"I paid for it. I've paid for all of it, everything. So shut the fuck up moaning. Some friend you are."

"I promised your mum I would look out for you, and I feel like I shouldn't be leaving tomorrow. How will you manage without me?"

Ellie stopped, turned around and faced Fi. She shook her head and tried to make sense of the words. Her face scrunched up tight before she erupted into laughter. "You. Looking after me. Oh my God. Seriously?"

She fumbled in her bra for the key, and jammed it in the lock of the door, leaving Fi to fight to remove and close it. Ellie scattered her clothes along the floor to her bedroom and swung open the balcony doors, where she set up a line of coke and snorted it.

"I'm here Dad. Right where I need to be. Don't worry – I will get what should rightfully be mine."

"Who are you talking to?" Fi stood in her bedroom doorway, unsurprised by Ellie's nakedness.

"Go to fucking bed, will you?"

Fi turned away and disappeared. She was so innocent, had absolutely no clue about life. A bad choice to have brought her, but then she had no other friends left. No one else around. Life was pretty shit, until her 21st. No party, nowhere to celebrate except some lame dinner with her mum and her stepdad and what was she going to do with a bracelet? But then her letter arrived. From her dad. Well not exactly from her dad, he was dead. But his solicitor, a firm her mum said were dodgy, no surprise there, nothing her dad ever did was up to scratch with her. Turned out, he had set up a trust fund to which she had access from her 21st birthday. A trust fund totalling £300,000.

She laughed as she remembered her mums face drain of colour, and reality dawn that she would no longer be able to control her; that he had given her utter freedom, to do whatever she wanted. She was in Spain within the month and set up various meetings to look at places to rent or buy. Holidaying was over, the next part of the trip was work. To lay her dads spirit to rest finally, and to claw back her fortune.

TATE

Tate arrived early at 'Miguel's', after the insistent message from Irena that they meet immediately on her return from Malaga. She had important news apparently, but Tate planned to use this quick drink to break the news about her plan to split with Mauricio too. Hopefully Irena wouldn't waste her breath trying to convince Tate to give him another go. She stirred the mojito with her straw and sucked out the ice which was stuck in the end.

She loved the dark wood and tropical feel of 'Miguel's. The artwork was funky and retro, and the velvet bucket seats a variety of colours. Huge potted plants dotted about gave the feel of privacy in a generally open plan space. This was her favourite bar. She rooted through her bag for her lip balm and felt grateful for the air conditioning which was already cooling her down. It had been a hot day. Even the three elderly gentleman in their striped shirts and fedoras, who whiled away their days in the shade of the citrus trees in the square, sought extra cover from the brutal sun. The square felt empty without them in their usual spot, watching the world go by and listening to the church bell chime every fifteen minutes. She took comfort that they hadn't gone far, if you looked carefully, you could spot them, sat together in the tapas bar. They were as much a part of the square as their worn bench.

"Is this seat taken?"

Tate looked up and locked eyes with the stranger, who smiled hopefully down at her.

"Yes, it is."

He looked puzzled, "it looks empty…."

"It is."

"Right, so shall I stay, or shall I go?"

Tate scratched her neck and stared at his blue eyes and the smattering of freckles across his nose. He swept his wavy hair off his face, and widened his eyes, awaiting an answer.

"Stay, I mean until my friend arrives at least." Her stomach turned over and she rubbed her blushing cheeks.

"Can I get you a drink? Leo and you are?" he stretched out his hand towards her.

"Tate," Her voice was raspy, and she shook his hand which gripped hers firmly.

"Well Kate what will it be?"

She sipped on her mojito and cleared her throat, "Sorry, it' s Tate not Kate…"

"Tate, right. Got it."

"Same again please." She smiled and watched him order their drinks. Who was he? Probably a holiday maker. Why hadn't she already split with Mauricio? Was he hitting on her? She hoped so.

Leo sat back down, "They'll bring them over in a sec. So, Tate, what's your story?"

"Oh, far too long and boring…I don't want to drive you away when we only just met, how about we start with you? Do you often approach women in bars and ask for their life stories?"

His laugh showcased a bright smile, and she wondered what it would be like to kiss that mouth.

11

"Oh yeh, whenever possible really." He turned to look up at the waiter, who was setting down their drinks on the small round table, "Thanks."

Tate stifled her excitement by sipping her drink and chewing her straw. "Haven't seen you here before."

"I haven't been here for a while, so that figures."

"So, you have been here before? Not on holiday then? Not been here for a while? How long are you here for?"

Leo laughed, "Wow, you talk fast."

Tate shifted in her chair, and silently berated herself for her lack of cool.

"Let me see, I used to live here, no I'm not on holiday and I am not planning on leaving for a while. Does that answer your questions?"

She nodded and chewed her lip. "These mojitos are strong I think."

He nodded and lifted his glass, "Cheers, to good times."

Their glasses chinked and they locked eyes as they took a sip.

"You staying nearby?"

"Very close by, so if you..."

"Tate!" It was Irena. Bloody hell. Bad timing.

"Irena," Tate stood up and knocked the table. Leo expertly caught her drink before it could spill over them both. "Well saved, thanks."

Leo bowed in response.

"Leo, this is..."

"No way! Leo? It's been years, how many, six or seven maybe?" Irena's face beamed.

"Seven and you look as gorgeous as ever, do you ever age at all?"

"Mountain air, must be. It's not from early nights and lack of partying, eh Tate?"

"Nice to see some things haven't changed around here." He pulled Irena close and squeezed her tight, "great to see you, it really is."

Tate sat down, was that jealousy which curled her lips? "Erm, hello – sorry to interrupt but you two clearly know each other, so how come you never mentioned Leo before?"

"You mean, she never told you about me?" His hands grasped his chest and he feigned heartbreak.

"I don't talk to you about everyone I ever met in my life Tate, so he never came up in conversation I guess, it's no big deal!"

"Double blow, not interesting enough to discuss..." Leo slumped into the chair and grinned at Tate.

"So where is Celeste?" Irena glanced around the bar and then focussed back on Leo.

Tate's ear pricked up and she felt a bit sick, please don't say he is married, or with someone.

"Ancient history, never made it to the alter, about two years ago since we split."

Tate let out a long sigh of relief and both Leo and Irena turned around.

"So, you've met Tate then," Irena tipped her head towards her, and Tate continued to twirl her hair around her fingers with her head leaning to the side.

"Uh huh," Leo answered directly to Tate, "but only a moment ago."

"Listen, before we catch up can you give me five minutes with Tate, I must talk to her about something."

"Sure, I guess I'll be over there." He took up his original position with a clear view of Tate and supped his drink. She could feel his eyes on her and despite her hot flush she plumped her lips and fiddled with her hair. Not looking over at him was almost impossible. She fixed her eyes on Irena's nose piercing.

Irena sat down, and took a deep breath, "I'm going to come out with this, because there's no easy way of saying it so, Mauricio is shagging around and why are you staring at my nose?"

Tate allowed the words to sink in, "How do you know?"

"I have my sources, someone out of town. When I went to Malaga today, I met an old contact, we had lunch chatted about life and she mentioned him. And before you ask, yes, it is him because she showed me a picture of them in a bar.

Sorry I pushed you and him..." Irena stopped; her brow lifted in confusion.

Tate was smiling, relief washed over her, this would make it easier.

"You're smiling because?"

"I was ending it anyway; you must have noticed that we aren't really getting on? Truth is, I should have binned him a long time ago, but it was easier not to, I guess. But now, he is driving me up the wall, so..."

"That explains the flirting." Irena tipped her head back towards Leo and smiled.

"What flirting?" Tate feigned shock, "Shush now."

"I guess the appearance of a certain new man is good, perhaps he can ease your pain, have you actually finished with Mau yet?"

"No, but I will. And there is no pain, I feel nothing, well maybe irritation, he is very irritating."

"Right, I need a drink, I've been worrying about how to tell you, for nothing!" Irena stood up and shouted towards Leo. "Does our catch up involve cocktails?" She kissed Tate and moved away towards her old friend.

"I'm off, I need to catch my cheating boyfriend before he goes off gigging. Nice to meet you, Leo." Tate leaned in and kissed him on both cheeks, inhaling his scent of Armani aftershave and lingering slightly longer than necessary.

"Wow, you sound chirpy considering…and the award for least angry cheated on girlfriend goes to…"

Tate smiled at him, "It was over way before this to be fair, I'm all good."

He kept hold of her hand, "Perhaps we might bump into each other again soon, especially now you are about to become single? My timing is spot on by the sounds of it."

"I hope so," Tate pinched Irena's bottom, "text you later but see you manana." As she walked away, she knew Leo was watching her and she left feeling powerful and full of hope.

The melancholic strumming of guitar filled the narrow street from the open window above, Mauricio was practising. She paused for a moment and listened, inhaling the scent of jasmine from the balcony opposite.   He sounded good, but his voice no longer had any effect on her. The music stopped with her closing of the door and his face peeked out from the top of the stairs, "Hey I've got twenty minutes, any requests?"

"We need to talk," Tate put her bag on the table and her keys on the rack.

"Oh, I don't know that one, who's it by?"

"Always such a comedian," she tied up her hair into a high knot and sat down.

"Is this about me waking you up, I had way too much rum…"

"Yes and no. You wake me up all the time." She crossed her legs. "You contribute nothing. This isn't working for me and its evidently not working for you either, after the information I've been given."

"Oh, she told you then. I thought she would. It was just sex you know." He pushed his hair off his face and shrugged.

"I want you to leave."

"Can I stay until I find somewhere else then?"

"A week tops. And no funny business. You can take the spare room."

"It really didn't mean anything to me...I don't even know her really..."

"Ah, well, that's ok then..." Tate shook her head, "FOR FUCKS SAKE, at some point you have to grow up, and while you're at it, get a proper job that actually pays you enough to live on..."

"Harsh, but while we are being honest, what did you expect me to do, you dried up months ago and I'm merely a man with needs..." He gesticulated with his hands, and this infuriated her more. It was all for effect, and she saw through all his bullshit.

Tate stood up and her face flushed, "Oh fuck off, get out of my sight. You have one week and then you're out. And don't keep waking me up coming in pissed or you'll be out sooner." She pushed past him into the kitchen and texted Irena: **ITS DONE, officially single,** before grabbing a cold water from the fridge. She hoped sharing this new information may encourage Irena's matchmaking obsession to kick in with Leo. Mauricio was right, she dried up months ago, and that needed to change.

Her phone pinged back immediately with a selfie of her and Leo. Tate slumped onto the chair and zoomed in on his face. Nice blue eyes, tousled hair, strong stubbly jawline…

"Tate, have you got a twenty I can borrow?" His hands were together as if in prayer.

She scrolled off the picture and reached into her bag for her purse, "Here's forty, that's the last you'll get from me, no more freeloading – go and get your shit together."

He nodded in resignation and pecked her cheek, "Thanks." He looked like a chastised school kid as he scuttled away.

She stood in the window and watched him wander along as though he had not one care in the world, whistling the evenings playlist as he walked. Nothing seemed to touch him. She sighed and wished she was made that way.

ELLIE

"Hey driver you've gone the wrong way. I said I needed to go to the town square in Campolita, you have passed the turning."

"Relax, here have this cold water, I know this area, been here for years. Just leave the directions to me, ok?"

Ellie took the water and drained the bottle, her hangover was rampaging through her body, and the winding roads were not helping. So far, she had avoided throwing up, for which she was grateful, as her taxi driver was hot. She pulled her new Ray-bans back onto her face and closed her eyes, drifting in and out of fitful light sleep. Fi would be on the flight home now, and it was a relief that she was no longer around to nag her.

The car stopped, "It's me, open up."

Ellie looked around and panicked. They were not at the town square but pulling in through some tall electric gates into a vast villa. The driveway was peppered with palms, and it swept around past the front of the house to the back, where a large parking area was bordered by shrubs and pink flowers. "What's going on? Who are you?" Panic rose and her throat constricted as she pulled at the door handle which failed to open. "Is this my dad's place? Are you taking me to him?"

"Shh calm down, you're safe and there is nothing to worry about. I don't know anything about your dad, but I am coming around to open your door, and I promise, nothing is going to happen."

Ellie struggled to control her breaths as the driver walked calmly around the car and smiled. He put his hands up to reassure his passenger and slowly opened her door. Ellie swung her legs out and stood up as she delivered a hard knee to his crotch, and a blow to his right cheek. She grabbed her handbag and ran back around to the driveway, kicking off her flip flops as she went. The gates up ahead were closed again and too high to climb, she was trapped.

Her feet bled from the gravel, but she was not ready to give in. She ran the perimeter of the walls looking for somewhere low enough to climb. She was a caged animal, being hunted. The silence was eery, and even though she could not see anyone else, she felt as though she was being watched. Out of breath, she slumped to the floor, her back against the whitewashed wall, defeated. Not much scared her, but her stomach was tied in knots as her mind played images of sex trafficked females she had seen on the telly. Is this why she was brought here? Stupid, stupid, stupid. She smacked at her forehead, annoyed that she had not even bothered to check whether the car which arrived for her had been a real taxi. All the warnings her mum had nagged her about, all the safety talks her mum had insisted on giving her...and somehow, she was now trapped inside a stranger's villa with no way out. She clung to her last hope, that her dad wasn't dead after all, and this was some elaborate plan to bring her to him secretly...

After a few minutes, a figure slowly walked across the grass between two palm trees towards her. He stopped to smell a flower and then continued until he loomed above her. She shielded her face as she looked up at him, but the bright sun made her eyes squint.

"So, the apple didn't fall far from the tree with you I see," the shadowy figure crouched down, "Am I safe or are you going to attack me too? Your crotch move seems to be your speciality."

He was in his fifties, maybe less, and his face had seen too much sun, it was leathery and slightly baggy. He was probably gorgeous when he was younger. His cold eyes narrowed as she stared at him and said nothing. The knot in her stomach constricted her breathing and her head swam with thoughts. Was he going to kill her? Why did he want her here? His arms rested on his bent knees and his clasped hands were still. Neither said a word. Her thoughts darted to her dad; he must be something to do with him...didn't her mum always tell her what a dangerous world he was from.

"I take it you knew my dad?" Ellie sounded more confident that she felt.

"Bill and me, hell of a lot of history. When I heard you were around, thought I owed him, better check in on you. Seems you have been acquiring a reputation along the coast."

Ellie inspected the soles of her feet. They were torn and weepy.

"Let's get you inside and cleaned up, that looks pretty sore."

"How can I trust you?"

"Well Ellie, you don't really have a choice right now. You can scream, but no-one will hear. You can run, but there's nowhere to run to, and your phone, well it's not in your bag." He pulled her iPhone from his trouser pocket and waved it at her. "You can have this back, but first, we're going to sort out your feet. Then you can hear what I have to say. We need to give my driver a little breather anyway, a little run in with a firecracker left him a little bruised shall we say." He smiled and grabbed her hands lifting her to her feet.

21

Ellies interest was piqued. He didn't seem so bad, and she did need to get her feet sorted out. "Okay, but I'm not staying long, I don't even know your name."

"Tony, and you're free to leave whenever you want as long as it's when I want you to leave."

Ellie limped alongside Tony, passed the swimming pool, which glistened and offered respite from the relentless heat. Under an archway past a huge table, two girls lay in bikinis on sun loungers. They looked like twins.

"Hey Tony," they spoke in unison.

"Viv, Leila, this is Ellie, Bill's daughter."

The girls sat up and swung their legs over the side of the loungers. They lifted their shades onto their heads and stared.

"What's happened to her feet?"

"I cut them, my flip flops came off, actually I need to find them, and I've dropped my Ray-bans – and they're new."

"Its fine, I will have someone pick them up for you, come on - this way."

Ellie caught the girls mumbling about her dad but could not quite catch what it was they said. Tony opened the door to a whitewashed stone building, and inside the plush Moroccan feel took her breath away. Huge sofas with cushions and throws, gold everywhere and tall lanterns. This is what she wanted her new place to look like. "Woah, this is lush," she imagined diving onto the sofas and jumping around.

"Girls?" He called towards the door in the corner, and three pretty girls ran in. "I need one of you to patch up Ellies feet and we also want some drinks, my usual and for you Ellie?"

"Erm, can I have a sex on the beach?"

Tony stifled a laugh and nodded at the girls who scurried away. Ellie's wide eyes absorbed the sumptuousness of the place.

"Sit, please," Tony moved some cushions to make a space for her to sit with her feet up at the end of the sofa so that they could be cleaned and dressed.

Ellie relaxed back and smiled as she gratefully accepted her cocktail. Another of the girls tended to her feet. It was strange, none of them spoke and she found it hard to make eye contact with them too. "Thanks," was all she managed once her feet were dressed, before they disappeared again.

"So, can you tell me about my dad?" she drained the last of her cocktail and placed the empty glass on the mirrored table next to her.

Tony sidled over and perched on the edge of the footstool in front of her, "What are your plans while you are here? Place to stay? Know anyone?"

"I've was on my way to pick up my keys to the rental I have lined up, but I sort of ended up here...I am looking to buy somewhere too. Dad left me a trust fund," she smiled.

"So, you've turned 21 then. I remember him setting that up when you were young. How time flies. And now you are here,

23

and he's gone. Life is a strange thing…" He gulped the re-maining whiskey and placed the empty glass on the floor.

"Another cocktail?"

Ellie nodded; this was the life. No wonder her dad had chosen to live out here, it beat the UK any day and the dull life her mum and stepdad led. "So, about my dad. Do you know what happened? I mean, it can't have been an accident. Surely someone did this to him?"

"Another cocktail," he ordered into the empty space of the room. Ellie half expected a puff of smoke and a magical ap-pearance. "Well, the question is, how bad do you want to know. I mean how far would you go to get it? I don't give information for free; you have to give me something in return." Tony's expressionless eyes bored into her.

Ellie felt the colour drain from her face, "I'm not fucking you if that's what you mean." Her shrill voice evidenced her panic.

Tony's laughter shook his body. Ellie laughed along with him, hoping this was all a wind up, until he turned and leaned in close enough for his nicotine breath to warm her face. "You don't give me orders little girl, and I fuck who the hell I want to. Nothing in life is free, and if you want something from me, then it's only fair I get something in return. You are one cocktail down, and let's not forget the injury you caused my staff member. I think that means you owe me already. Clear enough?"

Ellies wide eyes fought back the tears and with her shallow nod, he loosened the grip of her chin between his fingers.

A fresh cocktail was placed silently beside her, and the empty glass removed. The invisible girl did not flinch as Tony handed her his glass with one hand and smacked her bottom with the other, his eyes suddenly ignited by her scantily clothed body. He stood.

"Now, enjoy your drink and then we will take you to collect those keys," his friendly voice was back. "Remember Ellie, I know what you are doing, who you are seeing and where you are going. Carry on establishing yourself, and I will contact you. In good time I will give you the information you are seeking." Tony passed her the fresh cocktail and tossed her phone into her lap as he casually sauntered off towards the back, dropping his shirt to the floor and disappearing out of sight.

Bile crept up her throat. She put the drink back down on the table and shuffled off the sofa. The driver was waiting to take her into town, "Here, you dropped these." He handed over her now-scratched Ray bans and flip flops.

"Thanks. Oh, and I'm sorry I hurt you, I just, I mean, well, I was scared that's all."

He turned away in silent disgust as she hobbled back out past the empty loungers. Her legs shook, and her feet throbbed but most of all fear was shadowing her. What had she done? Why did she always have to get herself into bad situations. And what was Tony going to use her for? Fi was right after all, and she wished she had not sent her home.

TATE

With Mauricio gone, the house felt so different, lighter and spacious. In the end they parted on okay terms, but there was no love lost, and she was under no illusion that he would miss her money more than anything else.

As predicted, Irena had given Leo her number, and they began a barrage of flirty messages immediately. Now Mauricio was gone, she hoped to see Leo on a proper date. He was intriguing and there was a lot she still didn't know about him. She quite liked that, the air of mystery and the promise of seduction made her tingle in anticipation.

Her phone rang, "Hey Chica! Guess what? I have a surprise for you, you will not believe it. Don't go anywhere. I will be with you in an hour." Irena hung up before Tate could utter a response, but her stomach was already flipping at the thought of Leo. It must be connected to him; Irena was well aware of her feelings, and it was totally her style to match-make. Was that the door?

Tate popped her phone into her jean shorts pocket and sprinted down the stairs, but on opening the door there was no one to be seen. Out of the corner of her eye, she saw an envelope on the floor. She darted out onto the street to see if anyone was around, but it was empty and quiet, except for a stray dog hunting for scraps. The potted plant on her doorstep looked sad, and she couldn't remember when she last watered it, poor thing was withering in the heat. She tucked the envelope into her belt, it was bound to be some lame gesture from Mauricio, an apology or begging for somewhere to stay. She grabbed a jug and filled it with water from the kitchen.

"Sorry Mr Plant," she said as she saturated the dry earth, "I really will try to remember to water you in future."

"Hey, Mr Plant isn't looking too good, in fact I would go as far as to say he's been, well, neglected actually."

Tate knew the voice before she spun around, and her face erupted into a smile, "Well I've had other things on my mind. Mr Plant will make a full recovery, I'm sure."

Leo leaned in and kissed her cheek, "How's it going?"

Tate, aware of her scruffy appearance, tucked her hair behind her ears and pulled at her t shirt. "Bit hectic to be honest, work is manic, Mauricio has finally gone and now Irena is springing some surprise on me..."

"Intriguing..."

"Well, you would know, what are you two up to?" She playfully pushed his arm, and her body responded to his touch, by erupting in goosebumps.

His face screwed up in confusion, "Huh?"

"I assumed, it involved you considering..."

"Considering..."

Tate's face dropped, if it wasn't about Leo, then what was it? "Never mind."

"Hey, don't look so disappointed, you said Mauricio has finally gone." Tate leant back against the cool white wall and

Leo moved a step forward. He leaned in and whispered in her ear, "Which means you have an empty house right now…" His lips brushed her cheek and his aftershave tingled in her nose. She turned her head towards his face. As their lips grazed, her body jolted. He kissed her gently, and then deeper and she returned his kiss passionately before pulling her head back and gasping for air. A wooden shutter banged, and her elderly Spanish neighbour suddenly began to clatter on her balcony; her steely eyes watching their stolen kiss. She knew her loud tutting was because Mauricio only recently moved out, and that she was judging her.

"We can't do this, not right now, I told you Irena is on her way, and who knows what she has planned. Besides, we appear to have an audience." Tate nodded towards her neighbour.

Leo turned around, "Hola, Senora, it's a beautiful day, isn't it?" He waved and smiled as she scurried inside.

Tate pushed him back and laughed, "You are naughty!"

Leo took her hand and pulled her in close, but she couldn't trust herself with any more kisses, she already wanted to rip his clothes off.   He whispered, "Is it my eyes or has Mr Plant perked up already?"

She pushed him away, "Everyone knows your supposed to talk to plants! I'm not crazy."

His eyes lit up as he laughed, "Message me later and then we can resume where we left off." He kissed her hand.

She stood and watched his tall frame stroll down the street until he disappeared around the corner. Her stomach flipped and her mind already began to play out what would happen next, she felt so alive, and her head buzzed with excitement. The heavy blue door closed with a push of her back and as she leant against it the envelope dug into her skin. She removed it from her belt and ripped open the seal already cursing whatever it was Mauricio wanted. He was history now.

Tate,
You knew my dad, Bill, and I really want to meet with you.
Please can you come tonight at 8 pm to the Viewing point above town?
Please don't let me down, I really need your help.
Thanks, Ellie.

Tate folded up the letter and stuck it in her pocket. What was that about giving with one hand and taking with the other? Leo arrives and things are looking good, then out of the blue Ellie shows up. She shook her head and slumped in the armchair. Not even a contact number or address, so no way of agreeing another time.

Her phone beeped, it was Irena, she was five minutes away. Suddenly she was in no mood for surprises and weariness hit her. She heaved herself out of the chair and headed into the kitchen to make a coffee, maybe that would help keep her awake.

"Chica? I'm here!" Irena's excited voice echoed around the ground floor. Tate pressed go on the coffee machine and headed back into the dining room.

29

"MUM! What on earth..."

"Surprise! Come here and give your mum a big hug."

Tears pricked her eyes and overwhelming relief flooded her, it was as though she needed her right then but had not realised until that very moment, "It's so good to see you."

"Are those tears? Let me see." Irena leaned in and then whooped for joy, "I did it! I genuinely surprised you and so my mission is accomplished!"

"Hey! Don't you go disappearing, you can stay for dinner with us," Tate hugged her friend tight and whispered, "Thank you."

"Well, my love, I thought it was about time I visited your shop and Irena called me and said you were about to be living alone again so, I took Bella to Aunty Pat, I couldn't bring myself to take her to kennels, and got on a plane...here I am!" She hugged her tightly and gently rubbed Tate's back.

"I am blown away that you're here. Really, come on let's grab your things and settle you in the lounge, follow me, this way, up the stairs."

The three of them chattered excitedly up the stairs to the second floor, where the Juliet balcony doors were open and allowing a fresh breeze to flow through.

"This is exactly how I imagined it to look, I'm so glad I've finally got to see it. I hate not being able to picture where you are."

Tate beamed with pride, "I'm glad you like it. Hopefully you will like your room as much, although I will need to put some clean bedding on for you. Now sit here," Tate plumped the cushions behind her mum, and lifted her feet up onto the pouffe. "Perfect place to watch the world go by. Irena and I will put together a tray of snacks and tea, you must be peckish." Tate did not wait for an answer but pulled Irena back downstairs to the kitchen.

"What's going on? I know you are happy about my surprise, so what is it? Has something happened? Is it Mauricio?"

Tate shook her head and pulled out the folded letter, "Read this."

ELLIE

Ellie hated sitting and waiting, for anything or anyone. It was doing stuff she got off on, so she snorted a line of coke. Her visit with Tony weighed heavily on her, and for the first time in ages, she felt small and vulnerable. He wasn't someone you could mess with, and it was clear that he was in charge. Her feet were almost healed now, and her tan nicely even, but she was on edge and had bitten her nails to the quick.

So far, her instructions were simple: deliver note, meet Tate, unsettle her.

But that all seemed too simple for Tony, and he promised he had something big to tell her if she completed her side of the bargain. There was more to come, but the not knowing, did her head in. His villa, the money, the pool and the driver, it all seemed like a dream come true. What unnerved her was that once inside the grounds, there was no way out and it felt like you were being watched all the time. What about the girls, the faceless girls who serve him unquestioningly and, from what little she witnessed, in every way he demanded? She remembered his tight grip on her chin and his cold eyes piercing through her. She shuddered. He must have spies all over, because he said something about what she had been up to on the coast, so there wasn't much chance she could escape without his say so. For now, she would do as she was told, at least he hadn't forced her to stay at his villa, even if she was probably being watched all the time. One more line would loosen her up, so she sniffed two just to make sure.

At 7.45, she sauntered down the apartment stairs, and lit up a cigarette. The car was already waiting and the driver eager to make eye contact, which she ignored and studied her phone instead.

"About time," he mumbled as she slammed shut the car door.

"No point being too early, anyway."

They sat in silence for the rest of the journey, which suited her. The driver was still smarting from her crotch blow, and failed to hide his contempt, which she found funny. There was no time for small talk anyway as she needed to mull over the information Tony had given her about Tate. It was hard to know what to use, and how far to go. All she could hope is that when faced with her, she would know. She lit another cigarette, expecting the driver to complain and felt disappointed when he lit his own up instead.

He pulled up at the viewing point, "I will be back in ten minutes from when her car pulls up, so make sure you do what needs to be done in that time."

"Who put you in charge?" She fired back.

He said nothing. Ellie opened the door and slammed it hard before heading over to the bench.

It was a nice view, but she wouldn't travel miles for any view, and couldn't understand why anyone would. But you couldn't help but feel tiny, that part was true. She expected a few dog walkers to be around, but it should be relatively quiet by 8pm.

She turned her head with the slam of a car door and watched Tate walk towards her.

"Hi, Ellie?"

Ellie nodded and stared as Tate sat down beside her on the hot bench.

"Want one?" She offered Tate a cigarette which she took and lit from Ellies flame.

For a moment, the only sound was a distant car and a barking dog. The air was cooling to a comfortable temperature, Tate coughed as she inhaled.

"So, you were my dad's..."

Tate turned to face her words.

"What, exactly, were you? I mean girlfriend seems a bit far-fetched, but from the sounds of things you had crossed the line from whoring...so..."

"I don't know who you've been speaking to, but I loved your dad, and would have done anything for him."

"That's part of being a whore, isn't it? Working your tricks, pleasing your client, whatever they ask – do?" Ellie smiled. Tate shifted on the bench.

"You shouldn't be so judgemental; you never know when or how you might end up in desperate circumstances. Becoming a sex-worker isn't always about choices."

"I laugh when people call it sex-worker, it's like they try to dress it up, make it more presentable."

"Ellie, I hope we haven't come here to discuss my past career choices. Is there something you need to know, that I can help you with?"

"I came out here you know, right before he disappeared his boss Paul, brought us out here for a surprise. He couldn't get rid of me quick enough...too busy fucking about to spend time with me but you would know all about that."

Tate bit her lip, "Actually, he had good reason, it was to protect you."

"What happened to him? I mean, I think we both know he died in that fire, even if no one cares enough to investigate and give him a proper send-off...fucking joke. Protect me? Huh...he didn't care about me; otherwise, why wouldn't he have shared his life with me? Instead of thinking he could

34

throw me the odd festival ticket as some sort or compensation, he could have actually got to know me…even now, he is keeping me close enough to him by giving me money, and still, I KNOW NOTHING!"

"I don't know what you want me to say, I don't really know much about that fire. But he did love you, I think you were the only person he did actually love."

Ellie stubbed out her cigarette butt with her foot and immediately lit another up. She inhaled deeply and blew out a trail of smoke rings. "I don't understand something, how do you go from being a penniless whore, to owning your own shop? Co-incidence that it all happened around the time my dad mysteriously disappeared and Camino's bar, where he and Paul conducted business, burns to the ground, don't you think?"

Tate swallowed hard and reached inside her handbag for her bottled water. "Inheritance and yes co-incidence, not that I need justify myself to you."

"Did you know - a few things were overlooked at the time, like cameras, evidence. The Police over here may have swept stuff under the carpet, but what if they weren't the first to his villa, or to check the security cameras which he had installed, ironically, after you were attacked?"

Tate choked on her water.

"Well, that's it for now, but I'll be in touch." Ellie stood up and walked away towards her car, pulling up on the road. As she got in, she wound down her window and stuck up her middle finger. Her pulse raced and her hands shook as she dabbed at the foil and rubbed powder into her gums. Shit that was amazing, as she thought about the look on Tate's face. The driver sped through the twisting roads, and her laughter filled the car.

"Boss wants to see you before I take you home," the driver spoke at her.

"Great, bring it on. Wonder if he'll let me have a swim in his pool?" Ellie felt unstoppable, oblivious to her hyper-state.

They parked up in the usual spot, and she sauntered through the archway to the office. Tony leant in the doorway puffing on a cigar. His open kimono showcased his trim and tanned chest, still glistening from his recent swim and his shorts were drying quickly in the heat. She squinted. Maybe he was fuckable if you kept your eyes half shut. He moved to allow her entry and followed her inside.

"So, why do you want me to mess with her?" She knelt on the sofa.

"Why not?"

"Just seems like a lot of effort to me. I mean, all this time you had evidence but only now you act?"

"No effort at all, I've had an indulgent afternoon, and not lifted a finger. There doesn't always have to be good reason for fucking people's lives up."

Ellie gasped, "She stole my dads' money. That's reason enough for me. But you, I mean, what's your reason?"

"I told you, I can't really think of one." He moved towards her and lifted the strap of her vest top off her shoulder. He sighed and turned away. "Maybe it's a nod to the good old days, when Paul and I ruled the Costas. Or maybe it's because Bill fucked me over," His voice rose with every sentence, "or maybe it's because she got her life together and I hate that, people thinking they can leave their shit behind." His eyes bulged and his lips tightened around his teeth. "Any of those good enough for you?"

He wandered towards the back of the room where a large fully stocked bar stood, and opened a wooden cigar box, where pouches of white powder were stored. "Come here."

Ellie bounced across the room and stood next to Tony, looking longingly at the powder now expertly lined up on the counter.

"Two for you and two for me," he laughed.

Ellie lent forwards, but he pushed her back, "Hey, don't be greedy." His stare brought her back to the reality of her situation and she chewed her finger. Why was he giving her this? But the pull of the drugs was strong, and she snorted the powder, while he set up four more lines.

At some point someone had brought in cocktails and left them on the table, which she thirstily downed, all the time gazing at Tony, who became more appealing by the moment.

He wore only a pair of shorts now, his kimono sleeve trailed coke off the bar and so it was ripped off in temper. Ellie felt a familiar urge. Her eyes travelled to his chest and what was contained beneath his shorts, as he strode towards her. She reclined on the sofa and closed her eyes. Maybe Tony would be her protector, provider even? He could help revenge her dad's death. He was much older, but so what? Her mum would do her absolute nut, Ellie laughed. All those times she was told how like her dad she was, she may as well take the chance to live in luxury and be a kept woman. Even if Tony was old.

He climbed on top of her, held her arms above her head and ripped her knickers free with his other hand. Ellie's heart raced and her head felt swimmy as she glanced sideways into a vast floor to ceiling mirror. Tony obviously liked to see everything, and he smiled at her in the reflection and licked his lips. "So now we have established how far you are willing to go,"

He let go of her wrists and stood up. "You're not my type I'm afraid, too mouthy. Get up and straighten yourself out."

Ellie flushed and winced as she adjusted her clothes and covered herself.

"Only thing you have got going for you, is your lack of moral compass."

She had never experienced sexual rejection before, how dare he? Hurt and anger raged through her, and she shook, but said nothing.

"Take this," he handed her a rucksack from behind the bar, "Be ready at 4."

"4am tonight? To do what?"

Tony sidled up close and yanked her hair down until her face looked directly up at him. She gasped.

"I will send you further instructions, but until then, go home, take this and await my text. You really need to work on your vocal skills, always talking when you should be listening."

Ellie gave a tiny nod, and he loosened his grip, "Off you go."

TATE

Tate drove back towards town feeling messed up. The taste of the cigarette lingered, and she stuffed a handful of mints into her mouth. This business with Ellie could bring up so much shit from her past. Who was feeding her this information? It had to be Tony. He had been relatively quiet since the whole fire thing. At least, quiet enough not to be public news. But he was still a shadow, and if someone poked the nest, he was capable of stinging.

Ellie was a silly young girl, who needed answers about her dad, but she had no idea what she was getting involved with and who. It reminded Tate of herself when she first arrived in Spain, naïve and tunnel visioned. It was a lucky escape for her, but she had endured a lot in order to get to that point. Her past being raked up, meant she would have a lot of explaining to do. Would it affect her clients, if they found out she had been a sex worker? Yes. Would Leo run for the hills? Probably. But the newest arrival in town, that's what scared her the most, her mum. She would be bereft.

Fuck. She needed to think. One name sprang to mind. Celia. She had connections with Tony and was usually willing to help whoever paid her bills. She would contact her, see if she could find anything out. It had been a while since they chatted, and Tate hoped she would still be up for a challenge.

If Ellie was serious about getting money from her, and if she was anything like her dad, she would stop at nothing. It would mean giving up everything she had built. No, it would not come to that. It was a bluff and if Tony wanted her dead or ruined, it would have long since happened. There was more to this, Ellie was in more danger than she was.

Tate parked in the bays near her house beneath the row of citrus trees and checked herself in the mirror. She wasn't looking her best and drew her lip balm from the glove compartment, took her hair down from a messy bun, and shook it out. She needed distracting. Blood rushed through her veins with the thought of another deep kiss from Leo. It was unfinished business, and her burning desire built in the pit of her stomach as she sprayed perfume all over and took a deep breath.

Miguel's bar was buzzing, and she could hear the incomprehensible chatter from the end of the street.

"You seen Leo?" She called through the open window at Miguel's to the girl pouring a frothy beer from the pump. Her mouth watered.

"Sure," the waitress turned inwards and shouted, "LEO, someone for you!" She pointed outside.

"Hey you, you okay?" Leo leaned down and kissed her cheek, "Well Irena and your mum are inside, come in and join us..."

"What are they doing here?" She realised she had said this out loud and silently berated herself. "I thought you may want to see if we can resolve those loose ends from earlier?"

Leos eyes widened, and he took her hand, "Loose ends huh? Well, yes, I would feel happier if we could get those all tied up, I mean I always think it's best to resolve outstanding issues at the earliest opportunity..." he winked, a little tipsy. "You sure you're ok?"

"Yes, fine, I, I can't stop thinking about you." It was true, he was playing on her mind.

He pulled her in tight by cupping her face with his hands and stared into her eyes. Her body sprung to life and silenced her swirling mind as she leaned up onto her tiptoes and kissed him. Her hands gripped his shirt; her desire and need erupted like an overflowing river bursting its banks. He pulled back, held her at arm's length for a moment, his eyes questioned what she was doing, but her fast breathing prevented her from speaking.

"Shall we go back to my place, is that what you want?" He whispered and she nodded, but he was already fumbling in his pocket for his keys, whilst pulling her down the street towards his house.

The door barely closed behind them as his mouth hungrily found hers and her whirling mind was instantly replaced with a need for him. His mouth now on her neck and his hands fervently roamed her body, eager to touch every inch. She

41

ripped at her clothes and then at his, desperate to feel his firm skin against her own. He lifted her upstairs and their kisses deepened on the way to his bedroom. Leo gently laid her on the bed, and stood for a moment, staring at her naked body, but she pulled him down on top of her, and arched and moaned at his every slow and deliberate movement. Whatever this was between them, she wished it would never end.

Leo enveloped her with his arms and pecked tender kisses across her shoulders. Her irrepressible smile faced away from him. She needed this moment of closeness as much as the sex. Bill never spooned her, he was all about the sex, there was rarely after-intimacy. As for Mauricio, he was all about Mauricio. Now, to feel safe, wrapped up in Leos arms was a beautiful moment, which she burned into her memory.

"Will you stay tonight?"

"I can't, my mum has only arrived like five minutes ago, remember?"

"True," he pecked at her ear and neck. "I have heard some cracking stories about you."

Tate rolled to face him, "What sort of stories?"

"You sucked your thumb until you were twenty, maybe you still do? And you failed your driving test ten times before you passed, mental note not to let you drive me anywhere!"

"If I wasn't enjoying your naked attention so much, I would leave right now." She should have known her mum would happily tell all her secrets once Irena got the drink inside her. "How did you end up with them anyway?"

"Innocently eating some tapas, when I was accosted by them. Resistance was futile they told me, so I joined them. It was a great evening, but to be fair, it just got a whole lot better." He lent in and kissed her gently, "so are you going to tell me what's wrong? I mean I'm not complaining about being approached in the street by you and then being taken advantage of...."

She traced her finger from his lips and neck slowly down to his stomach. His chest, still pale from his recent arrival was firm with a smattering of fine hair. She nuzzled her nose into it and snuggled as close as she could get, "I wish I could stay."

His hand rested on her bottom, "how long have we got?"

"Maybe an hour? Cannot imagine they will be out too late."

"You could always blame me. I think they would both approve of this, whatever this is."

"Maybe I should go now, my sensible head seems to have returned, I'm sorry. I mean, I don't usually do things like this..."

"You said an hour..."

"You really don't understand how much I wish I could stay," she hunted around for her clothes which seemed to litter all the way to the front door. "At this rate I will be here until next week, where are my knickers?"

Leo pulled them out from beneath his back, and dangled them in the air, "Come and get them…"

"Seriously, hand them over…"

"Nope."

"Well, then I will have to walk home commando style. It wouldn't be the first time; in fact, I quite like it."

Leo rolled onto his side and leaned on his elbow, watching her dress, "I usually prefer watching the undressing part better, but this is really fascinating."

"Last chance to give up the knickers," she outstretched her hand, her other on her hip.

"Okay. Here," he threw them towards her, and she caught them and swiftly put them on and her shorts on top.

"So, a love em and leave em type, eh?" He sidled up behind her and wrapped his arms around her waist, she leaned her neck to the side and as he nibbled her ear, her breathing sped up. She fought the urge to turn around and push him back onto the bed, reluctantly removing his arms from around her.

"You, are a naughty boy and I need to go, you're making this really difficult for me."

He nodded, "Well give in and come back here then. At least for half an hour?" He hopped back onto his bed and yawned, "Tate, where did you go earlier?"

Tate closed her eyes tight and tried with all her might to be sensible and to go home. But seeing him naked, his hands

44

behind his head, smiling at her, changed her mind. She slipped back out of her shorts, down to her bra and knickers, "Move over then, I'm coming back."

ELLIE

Ellie slung the rucksack Tony gave her over her shoulder and winced as it caught her sunburn. She hurried along the moonlit road, hoping the stray dogs would be the only encounters she would have. The square was swept clean, and the rubbish bags left out for the early morning refuse collectors who were due any time soon. She must be quick, and she played over his message in her head, what exactly he wanted her to do. She turned up the incline towards Bazaar and looked all around to check she was not being watched. It was silent.

She swung the bag from her back and shook the red spray cans, flinching with every click which echoed through the quiet. She reached up, and began to spray the shutters and walls, of the florist, careful as instructed, not to damage Irena's part of the shop. It was finished in a minute, and she was on her way back to her waiting car, around the corner.

Her head pounded. She longed for her bed, climbing wearily into the car, she lit up a cigarette. Two days of coke over-indulgence. Closing her eyes to the rhythmic move-ments of the car, she reflected on the last few days. Her dad would be royally fucked off about her even considering sex with Tony. She flushed with embarrassment at his rejection. Her wrists still hurt a little from his grip, and on reflection, perhaps it was a lucky escape. In the cold light of day, he really was the old man she first thought he was, but that's what drugs do to you – addle your brain.

The car stopped and she heaved open the door and slumped out. The stairs felt like a mountain, and she climbed them slowly, stopping on each one for a breather. She was going to sleep for a week, when she finally got into bed. Her door was ajar and suddenly adrenaline fuelled her weary body.

"Hey who's there?" She pushed the door fully open and reached in for the light switch.

"It's a friend. No need to worry." The thick Spanish accent did not sound alarming, and yet the hair on the back of her neck stood up as she searched his face, she had seen him some-where before.

"Who are you? What do you want with me?"

He wobbled as he stood and stumbled towards her. "I will scream this place down if you come any closer...back up there, fella." He looked as though he would crumple to the floor at the slightest touch and her fear was replaced with curiosity. He was in his 60s, and he was dishevelled.

"I don't want to frighten you. I'm sorry, I shouldn't have come."

"You don't get to leave because you say sorry, you broke into my room? Where I come from people don't do that for no reason."

His head dropped into his hands, and he rocked back and forth.

"I'm waiting…"

"I knew your dad."

"How?"

"I ran a bar…"

"Caminos? That's it you were the bar man!"

"You remember me? I was a nothing. They treated me as though I was invisible. But I saw things…you must understand, depraved things, things that haunt me."

"What do you know about my dad? Who torched your bar? Who killed him?"

"I know that they were setting up for young girls to carry their drugs for them. I know that they brought you here, that your name was on the list."

"Shut your fucking mouth old man. My dad was many things, but he would never EVER do that to me. Now get the fuck out of here before I call someone who will get you out of my room in a not so nice way, you understand?"

"You have to listen to me, please, I need you to…"

"Did you hear me? GET OUT." She grabbed his stained shirt and yanked him out of her door. He fell out on the floor of the landing, and she slammed the door shut, locking it. She watched him stumble down the stairs wailing, through the spy hole.

47

What the fuck was happening to her? Her adrenaline waned and she crawled into her bed. Before her mind could process any of the shit which her life seemed to be descending into, she passed out cold.

***

Her phone rang and woke her up. She had five missed calls, all from Tony and it was only 6.30am, only two hours of sleep. There was a message from her mum, desperate for reassurance that all was well, but she ignored and deleted it. Her claggy mouth felt disgusting, and she blindly reached for her water bottle, but it was empty. She launched it across the room and rubbed her pounding head. The phone rang again, "Yes."

"I've tried reaching you for 2 hours and was about to send the boys in, lucky you picked up."

"I was sleeping Tony."

"When I ring you answer."

"I was asleep."

"Said that already. What did the old man want last night? What did he say?"

"If you knew he broke in, why didn't you stop him?"

"I told you I was watching, not protecting you, that's not on me."

"Well, I didn't give him a chance to say anything, kicked him out. The florist job went well."

"Easy job, difficult to fuck up. Lay low, keep your mouth in check and I will be in touch." He ended the call.

"No problem your highness, I shall await your instructions, for fucks sake, I feel like a prisoner."

She headed into the kitchen and opened the fridge; the milk was off and the bread mouldy. Even her foils were empty, and she licked them clean, screwed them up into a ball and threw them against the wall.

If her shower revived her enough, she would head out for lunch and to score some more coke. She peeked through the blind. The car was parked opposite again and seemed to have become a permanent thing. The guy looked up towards her. She poked out her tongue and flashed her boobs. Prick.

TATE

Tate stretched out her legs and reached her arms above her head. She blinked open her eyes and struggled to focus but she was pretty sure that this wasn't her bed, she was still at Leos. Fuck. What about her mum? What about work? Where was Leo? Her watch calmed her down, it was only 6.30. Leo was an early riser. She tugged at the sheet and wrapped it around herself, "Leo?" she called, but the moment the word left her mouth, she noticed the note stuck on the mirror –
Gone for a run, back before you know it x

She headed into the en-suite and turned on the shower. His bathroom was sparkling, he must have a cleaner, she thought. She hung up the sheet on the back of the door and grabbed a neatly folded towel from the shelf, which she placed on the stool next to the shower. Relieved to see a selection of toiletries, she picked a shampoo conditioner and shower gel. They were high end, the type you got in spas and posh hotels, and smelled divine. The shower was powerful and pounded her skin, she climbed out feeling fresh and ready for the day.

She leant forward and towel dried her hair. "Well, that's a view I wouldn't mind seeing more of." A sweaty Leo lent against the door frame and clearly liked what he saw. "Glad you made yourself at home…"

"You don't mind, do you?"

"God no." He sidled up behind her, his shorts straining from his arousal, "I need to take a shower, but don't get dressed yet, it's still early, and I want to enjoy a coffee in bed with you."

"Coffee? Is that what we're calling it?" Tate kissed his cheek, "Have you got any deodorant?"

"Sure, in the drawer in the bedroom." He closed the shower door.

Tate rifled through his chest of drawers, and her eye caught a framed picture on a shelf above. It was of a beaming Leo cradling a baby. It reminded her that despite their comfortability with one another, there so much they didn't know. He knew nothing about her past with Bill, and clearly, she knew little about him. She didn't even know what he did for a living.

Leo wandered through, with his towel wrapped around his waist, "You looking at this?" He grabbed the framed picture and handed it to her.

Tate nodded, "I'd be lying if I said it hadn't caught my eye. Is the baby yours?"

Leo sat on the bed, and patted it for her to join him, "My little brother, big age gap, he's ten. Dad remarried a much younger woman. You look relieved," he grinned.

"It wouldn't have changed anything if he was yours, I like how this is going…I feel like we have known each other forever in some ways, and yet we have so much to learn."

Leo took the frame from her and set it back on the shelf. As he turned, he knelt on the floor and kissed her hands, and then gently parted her legs, "We have so much time," he said. And as he licked the inside of her thighs, she moaned and dug her fingertips into his thick wavy hair.

***

They sipped their coffees and exchanged smiles. Tate wished she didn't have to leave and was so glad she had unintentionally stayed over. "So, you really did want us to have coffee in bed together."

51

"Of course, a couple who coffees together, stays together."

"You made that up." She laughed, "Are you working while you are out here?"

"Erm, yes...are you being serious?"   His furrowed brow peeked over the rim of his coffee cup.

"What? I don't know what you mean?"

"Miguel's...where we met."

"You work in Miguel's?" Suddenly the penny dropped, as he always seemed to be there.

"Well sort of. You could say that. Miguel's is mine. Had managers in for a few years, but it's my bar, and I came back to run it myself. I mean, it runs itself mostly, my staff are great. But the official side, well..."

"No way. How did I miss that?" she shook her head, "I must have too much on my mind."

"Talking about that, what about last night, where did you go?"

"Just a ghost from the past. Will you walk with me to work then? I'm going to message Irena."

"She knows you are here, I messaged her before I went for my run. This ghost, is it a man?"

Tate grabbed his hand and looked directly into his eyes, "No, there is no one else, I told you, I really like you, this...."

"Okay. Good, let me throw some clothes on and I will come with you."

Tate texted Irena a row of smiley faces and hearts and a 'see you at work'. She wasn't at all   concerned that either her mum or Irena would be angry that she stayed out, they would both be pleased for her. Leo sprayed on his aftershave and threw on a polo shirt and shorts. He 'bryl-creamed' his hair and was ready before Tate managed to hook up her bra. She didn't mind the fact that Leo seemed to study her every move, in fact she revelled in his attention, which was usually followed up with some level of affection. It was everything she could want so far, and her smile was irrepressible.

"Have we got time for a quick coffee? Here I mean." Leo hovered in the door to the kitchen, "It's as good as any café round here..." he crossed his fingers.

"Okay, I could do with another, and I take it you really mean actual coffee?" Tate enquired.

Leo nodded, "on this occasion, yes."

 "Your kitchen is sparklingly clean, please make sure you give me warning before you visit mine. I need a team in to polish it all up!" She couldn't resist his hopefulness and cute face-squashed up awaiting her answer, "Okay just one coffee then, and you've really built it up now, so it had better be good!"

"Sit here, senorita," he pulled out a stool and she leant on the breakfast bar opposite where he   expertly navigated a complex looking coffee machine.

"Thank you, so you're a barista then, too?"

"Of course, I worked many a coffee machine before I set up Miguel's. Expert barista me," he placed a steaming milky coffee before her, "Would you like a sprinkling of chocolate?"

"No thanks, wow, you weren't lying, this is delicious, aren't you full of surprises."

"Good ones too, I hope," he raised an eyebrow.

"Wish we could spend the whole day here, just in a little 'us bubble', know what I mean?" Tate revelled in his company. He seemed considerate but funny and sexy as hell. She flushed as an earlier flashback popped into her mind.

Leo crept around the breakfast bar and leant in for a kiss. A sweet, gentle kiss, not deep and sexual like earlier, "I feel the same."

"Well let's cheers, to many more 'coffees' together," Tate lifted her mug and Leo chinked his against it.

"Whatever 'coffee' means," his eyes widened, and he winked.

***

They casually strolled towards the shop, their hands locked, both prolonging their parting.

"I've got a feeling I will be needing a lot of flowers for the bar, know any good florists?"

Tate laughed as her phone rang, it was Irena, "Hola," Tate sang, unable to contain her delight.

"Are you on your way to the shop?" Irena's voice was serious, something was wrong. They were already at the square and Tate could see a crowd around her shop front in the distance. She ended the call and broke hands with Leo, picking up her pace to a run.

"Tate- What's up?" Leo called after her and ran to catch up.

But she didn't stop or look back, something was wrong with the shop and as she neared, the crowd silenced and dispersed. Irena stood with a bucket and scrubbing brush, her hands-stained red.

The words: DIRTY MURDERING WHORE had been sprayed in red paint across the front of her shop. Leo caught up, "What the fuck?"

"My Mum, has she seen this?" Irena slowly nodded and pointed inside, "she's making the coffee."

Leo stepped in and shooed away the remaining onlookers, "Nothing to see, please off you go. Now leave this to me, you two. I've got contacts in the cleaning business; we can have this tidied within the morning. Go inside with your mum, Tate, I'll be in with Irena in a minute." Leo took charge and squeezed her hand.

Tate wandered despondently into the shop, as Leo called his cleaning contact. Her mum was busy making drinks and sorting out the ribbons into colours. "Oh honey, who would do that to you and what does it mean?"

Sobs escaped from her chest, and she was struggling to switch from the ecstasy which began her day to the drama now unfolding.

"Come here," her mum hugged her tight, swiped a tissue from her sleeve and wiped her nose and eyes. "Have this sweet hot drink, for the shock. Irena said Jo is off today, so I'm staying to help you all day. People are vile, aren't they? Ruining things people work so hard to create, how dare they?"

Tate could not speak, she nodded. Vile indeed. A vile act, by a silly young girl, Ellie. Her mum was now amid everything she had tried to keep from her. All the lies, all the years of pretence, that her life in Spain was wonderful, was for nothing, if she couldn't get a grip on this spiralling situation. Her poor mum could never comprehend what she had been through. It would devastate her. As for her clients, how would they take this? All this time, building up a good reputation, supporting the   community, floral arrangements for the elderly and bouquets rewarding the deserving of the town...now could be destroyed in one act. She had to brave it out, pretend it was mindless and puzzling.

Three amazing people, circling her, showing up for her. Offering support and practical help, as guilt ate away at her soul. Two of those people were completely oblivious to the truth. Her truth. Would they be offering their love and support if they knew everything? It was too much of a co-incidence for this to be happening days after Ellie's arrival, for it not to involve her. But Ellie didn't scare her, in fact she was scared for Ellie, because someone else was lurking in the shadows, she was sure of it. And his name sent shivers down her spine. Tony.

She couldn't imagine what conversations this would lead to with Leo, however she had to face facts that it wouldn't be long before he heard about her past...would he be so keen then? What an abrupt end to a perfect morning. Story of her life.

ELLIE

Once again, Ellie was on her way to Tony's. The only silver lining was the drugs she would be sure to get her hands on. At least he had made it clear that she wasn't on his radar for sex, which was something. This time she wore her bikini beneath her skirt and vest, ever hopeful that she would final-ly get some down time in the pool, she was following his instructions after all.

"Boss is otherwise engaged right now, so wait here." The driver disappeared into the accommodation over the sprawling garages. The cicadas silenced with her every move, and it was eerily quiet, even the twins weren't in their usual spot. She wandered around the courtyard, and stared longingly at the pool, which seemed to call her. Even the shade of the trees brought no relief from the   relentless sun. She had to hand it to him, his questionable career had brought him a fantastic   lifestyle, and his gardens were immaculate. Through the gate and around out of sight, stood the biggest hot tub she had ever seen, at least ten people could fit in it. She longed to immerse herself beneath the bubbles and sip a cocktail. Perhaps if she could prove herself, she would get to enjoy it some time? Who was she kidding?

Sun loungers lay empty, dotted around the pool, and it was almost like visiting a hotel or spa, rather than a private residence. She perched on the edge of the closest one to the diving board, and then moved to the edge of the pool where she sat and cooled her feet. The lure of the water was too tempting, and she whipped her vest and mini skirt off and slipped quietly in. Ellie ducked beneath and immediately felt her temperature cool. Floating outstretched on her back, she stared up at the cobalt sky. Lush.

The sun beat down onto her tanned skin, and she closed her eyes. If Fi could see her now. She remembered their short stay with her dad, back before... Fi thought his villa was amazing and that was half the size of this one. She cringed at her childish behaviour back then, and how her dad struggled to keep her in line. How did he expect her to behave when she barely saw him, resentment creeped back into her tummy like someone twisting her intestine, and her heart rate increased. She inhaled deep and exhaled slower, to bring her racing thoughts back in check. Her dad would not ruin this one moment of calm, in what had proved so far, a shit show.

She wished for access to a pool more often. Perhaps she could find an apartment with a shared pool, maybe even get back to her proper swimming. As a child, she was always swimming, and got as far as representing the county. But that was before her involvement with blokes, fags and coke.

Suddenly her head yanked back under the water, something tangled around her neck, and she grappled to free herself and resurface. Swallowing water, panic set in and she rolled and wriggled trying to breathe. Her fingers caught hold of what felt like a net, and it pulled her towards the side of the pool. A hard thud of her head on the tiled edge, caused a swirl of blood, and her hands gripped the metal ladder and propelled her up spluttering and choking.

Clambering onto the tiles around the pool, she choked and gasped for air. Suddenly aware of a   figure towering above, a glance confirmed it was Tony. He held a pool cleaning net, now ripped and torn from her struggle.

His face twisted in rage, "this is not a fucking hotel; you don't use the facilities without being invited. Get up and get inside."

Ellie shook, and struggled to stand, coughing prevented her from answering him, but she managed to follow him inside. Her hair streaked with blood which dripped down her face, and, once inside the cool of the aircon made her shiver even more.

"Take your clothes off," Tony ordered.

Ellie stood still, her wide eyes searching his face for some explanation.

"I said, take your clothes off. And don't sit down, or you'll spill your blood everywhere," he turned towards the bar.

She slipped off her bikini and covered as much as she could of her body with her arms, whilst he faced away.

Tony stood and sipped his whiskey for what seemed like hours, as Ellie awkwardly shivered.

"I'm so cold," she whispered.

Tony reached into a large basket on the floor and threw her a towel. She grabbed it gratefully and wrapped it around herself, relieved to be covered up, but still aware of her nakedness.

"You have much to learn. You don't get to do whatever you want in my house. You were told to wait for me, not swim in my pool. What an entitled young woman you are."

"I'm, I'm sorry," she whispered, "can I grab my clothes and put them on?"

Tony's gaze felt as though it would penetrate her skin. He nodded and she darted out to the pool and threw on her clothes. What was she thinking? Why did she think it was ok to do that? Maybe he was right, she really did have a lot to learn, and she needed to start right away.

This time there was no aftercare on offer for her injuries, the blood congealed into a scraggly mess in her hair. She caught sight of herself in the large mirror next to the bar, which seemed to reflect every dirty deed which played out. The confident, fearless woman she arrived as, was replaced with the reflection of a wide eyed, scrawny ghost-like figure. She turned away in disgust and wiped the blood from her face with the corner of the towel, "So, what next?"

Tony leaned against the mirror, forcing her to look towards it and smiled. "I think you should have a little chat with Leo."

"Who?"

"Tate's boyfriend, stir it up a bit. You know, you're looking for information about your dad...his ex-whore owns a florist..."

"They will know I graffitied the shop if I do that," Ellie shoulders dropped in defeat.

"And?" Tony's stare made her shiver.

"Well, isn't that a bit obvious? What if they report me? I still don't get what this is all for? I want the money she took, and to find out if she killed my dad, that's all."

"And I want you to do as you're told. I don't owe you anything, remember you OWE ME," his sudden aggression made her jump, his fists clenched.

Ellie nodded profusely, eager to appease. What was his motive? Why was he encouraging her to fuck Tate over?

Tony spun around and reached into the wooden box on the bar, "Here," he threw a small plastic pouch of white powder at her. "All you need do, is whatever you are instructed, and all will be clear, eventually."

She smiled, dabbed her finger inside and sucked it, sighing gratefully, she stood up. He was saving her a fortune by giving her the stuff, but the prospect of living under Tony's shadow forever wasn't too appealing, and Spain was growing less attractive with every interaction she and he had.

"Now clean yourself up and go," he instructed, "without dripping any more blood on my floor."

***

Ellie called the estate agent and cancelled her viewings. Once she cleared up the money situation and got the truth about her dad, she was heading back to the UK. For now, Tony was useful as her supplier and with getting even, but that was it. She hopped in the shower and washed the blood from her hair as carefully as she could manage. The sting of the shampoo made her wince, but she needed to get ready for her impending visit to Miguel's. Hopefully the welt on her head could be hidden by her hair, but it probably needed a stitch.

She clicked her neck and inhaled deeply. At least with this instruction she could enjoy some cocktails at the same time, it may even be a good evening...although it could go in a completely different   direction, and she may end up being driven away by the police, if they suspected her of the shop graffiti. Oh well, she had little choice if she wanted answers. She dried her hair and lay down for a nap before heading out for the evening.

TATE

Leo had come good with his promise, but the shop ended up being repainted, as the red paint would not shift. Her mum seemed to accept the suggestion that it was mindless graffiti, but she and Leo were yet to have a conversation, alone, about it all. She was dreading it. Leo was covering shifts at the bar, due to holidays, and she was avoiding going in there for now. He clearly got the vibe, and was relentlessly texting, at least he was still keen.

Jo had been amazing in the chaos of the last few days, and innocently fended off any questions   directed at her about what happened. Tate kept busy out the back, happy for Jo to maintain a cheerful front of house.

She checked her watch, it was almost closing time, she shut early on a Wednesday, and it was Jo's half day. Perfect time to make a call to Celia.

As Irena made the coffee, she rifled through the contacts box, and pulled out a piece of paper with Celia's number, and hoped it was still in use. It had been two years since they last met up in the UK. It rang.

"Hello," It was her, thank God.

"Hey Celia? It's Tate."

"Hey you, how's life? You still doing ok?"

"All good thanks. How's Keira?"

"Oh, she's growing up fast, making me feel old."

"Can't imagine you will ever look old…"

Celia laughed, "I guess there's a reason for this call? I mean, it's not like we're in constant touch?"

Tate cleared her throat and nodded at Irena, in thanks for the steaming coffee she placed in front of her, "You're spot on actually."

"Okay, so?"

"You still have contacts in Tony's world?"

"I thought the deal was, you give him a wide berth? Keep out of his way? Why you asking?"

"Trust me, I don't want anything to do with him, and I would gladly never see him again, but it seems the past has coming knocking at my door…Bill's daughter – Ellie."

"Ah."

The conversation stopped. Neither said a word.

"I suggest you ignore whatever is going on, fob her off, but stay clear."

"That sounds like a warning."

"I'm telling you for your own good, some things should be left alone, and, on this occasion, my   advice is, whether I have connections to Tony or not, you need to steer clear."

Tate sipped the coffee and shrugged her shoulders at Irena's inquisitive eyes.

"So, you won't help me?"

"Look Tate, no good can come of this for you. That's all I'm saying."

"Right, okay, tell me, if I can't ignore it, and if I need your intel, are you willing to help?"

A long pause gave Tate the answer she feared.

"You chose to stay in their world Celia. I didn't, and I don't, but my hand is being forced."

"You may want to get off your high horse Tate, you built a whole life with money earned in 'that world', don't forget it. I must go, Keira is calling me, I'm sorry."

The phone clicked off and Tate threw it down in disbelief on the counter.

"She basically told me to steer clear, and that she wouldn't help me. So that's that then."

"Well, I think maybe she's right. Ellie is a silly girl poking around things she has no idea about. We need to warn her off and forget about it all. The last thing you need, is to become re-acquainted with Tony. It's taken you long enough to build a new life, and what about Leo? How would you explain yourself? He's not stupid, and Tony has been around for a long time, so Leo is already aware of him and what he is capable of. You will have put Leo on his radar too, if you get involved now."

"I think she knows something and doesn't want to tell me."

"I expect she knows a lot, but why would she tell you anyway? She's not your friend. Being your friend is hard sometimes, you never listen, I don't think you are listening now even." Irena's irritated voice raised to a shout.

"I wonder what it is…"

"Jeez, you need to lock up and go see your mum. I don't know what to do with you anymore." Irena wandered back into her section of the shop and pulled the dividing curtain down between them. Tate locked up her door and cashed up, it had been a slow day and takings were down.

Celia's warning rang in her ears. She reflected on their meetings on her return to UK after her escape. They had initially thought they may set up in business together, honey-trap female fix-its. But it petered out, as they realised, they could never be more than acquaintances. They were from two different worlds. Tate fell into the underbelly of crime, and wanted to escape, but Celia married into it, enjoyed the fruitful trappings which it brought to her table. You couldn't take away from her that she was a great mother, and wanted a good life for Keira, but she seemed blind to the fact that blood money was never the right thing for paving a child's future.

It turned out, that she was staying at Tony's at the time she was photographed with Bill. Tony paid her handsomely to flirt and lead him on, having known and respected Celia's late husband. He was happy to help her revenge Bill, who had been involved with her husband's death. Tate wanted to break all ties with that world, but Celia couldn't quite manage it, the money paid too well and the lifestyle she loved wasn't afforded on a normal 9 to 5 wage. So, they gave up on the idea, and went their separate ways. There was no love lost between them, but equally they were not enemies.

Celia must know something. But her loyalties lay with Tony, by the sounds of it.

Tate gathered her bag and keys, and carried her takings through the curtain to Irena, who was busy serving a holiday maker. Tate slumped in the sumptuous armchair, which she hoped would never be sold, and waited for Irena to finish wrapping the gifts purchased by the ageing lady, who seemed in no hurry to leave, and happy to linger in Irena's warmth.

"I thought she would never leave," Tate handed the bag of takings to Irena to lock in the safe.

"She was a paying customer and has been in many times before, why say that? The universe doesn't revolve around you all the time." Irena, sighed.

Tate chewed her lip, she didn't like being told off by Irena, "Don't be like this, let's have a drink after I have been for dinner with my mum?"

"Won't you be seeing Leo?"

"We can all have a drink together, can't we? He is working tonight anyway. So…"

"Maybe, I have a headache now, so text me later and I will see if I am up to it."

Tate leaned in and kissed her on the cheek, "I do listen to you."

Irena turned and busied herself with the keys.

"Okay, so I'll see you later?"

Irena shrugged and continued to fumble with the safe. Tate left the coolness of the shop and stepped out into the busy plaza, and the heat of the afternoon. The tables beneath the shade of the canopies were mainly full of families eating and enjoying ice cold drinks. She wandered past and headed towards home and her mum. What was she going to do, if Ellie really didn't give up about the money? Most of it was invested, or in Jose's case, drunk. She had some left in the bank, as a buffer and could offer that if push came to shove, but giving up the business or the house, really wasn't an option. How could Ellie prove that they were bought using Bill's cash? What did she know? Nothing. She could explain that Jose had most of it, and she kept the smaller amount. For now, she would wait, until her hand was forced.

ELLIE

Miguel's was nicer than she imagined, and she sized Leo up as she ordered her first drink, "Sex on the beach please."

"Coming right up, choose a seat and I will bring it over," he offered.

"I'm fine here, I'll just perch."

"Meeting someone?"

"Nope."

"Then here is probably the best place to sit," he answered. "It's a friendly place and a pretty girl like you is bound to find someone to chat to, we're a friendly bunch."

She smiled and watched as he expertly put together her cocktail and place it down in front of her on a fresh bar mat, "Five euros please."

She reached into her purse and handed over a ten, "Keep the change."

"You'll be skint if you do that too often, here," he handed her back five euros and moved on to serve the next customer. She scowled at his rejection, and assumption that she was simply another tourist. She could wait. She downed the cocktail, "Another please."

"Wow you're a quick drinker, sure, one minute." His phone beeped and he checked it and put it back in his pocket. "Now, one more cocktail coming your way."

She stared at him, he was good looking, she could see the appeal. "You worked here long?"

"Long enough. It's my bar actually and I'm a bit rusty, haven't covered any shifts for a while. Only covering whilst someone is off, but it's good in a way, getting back into it, seeing what can be improved, what people like. Here." She took the cocktail from him.

"Thanks," She handed him another five euros.

"You like it in here? Anything you don't like?"

She looked around, it was trendy and clean and had a good vibe, "The music, maybe turn it up a bit?"

He laughed, "Right, I keep it lower usually so people can talk, but later in the evening it cranks up, the more people drink the more they want to dance."

He turned back to the waiting customers, and she realised that she was only going to get snippets of chitchat with him as the bar was filling up. She headed to the ladies, where she took a hit of coke from her bag and reapplied her lipstick. She looked better today, less ghost like and more surf chick. Today she liked her reflection, and she readjusted her vest top to show more cleavage.

Back at the bar, a young man sat on the stool next to her drink, "This is Sam." Leo pointed to the blonde lad who smiled at her. Great, so now he was fobbing her off with some lame holiday   romance. Although, he was her type and she hadn't had any action since leaving the coast, so maybe she could afford to loosen up a little.

"Hi Sam, nice to meet you." She smiled and lent over to scratch her leg affording him clear view of her bra-less chest, then hopped up on the stool next to him. "What are we drinking then?"

"Whatever you want?"

"Two more cocktails please, when you're ready Mr barman, I think Sam is paying." She winked at her new friend and tapped his knee.

"So, you on holiday then?" Sam chirped.

"Sort of. What about you?",

"Yep. What do you mean sort of?"

"Well, I'm looking for something really. A bit of a quest. Anyway, that can wait, at least until we get better acquainted."

Sam beamed, and nodded, "What did you have in mind?"

"Let's see where the evening takes us, who knows what will happen once I get a few cocktails down me."

***

Sam became more boring with every drink she downed. As her visits to the ladies increased, she became less steady on her feet and her voice grew louder. After the sixth cocktail, she struggled to get back on her stool, and Sam helped her up.

"You've got something on your nose," he pointed to her face.

She wiped it away with the back of her hand as his face registered what the multiple loo visits were about, "It was great to meet you Ellie, but I really have to go now." He was out of the door before she even registered what he said.

"Leo, where did he go?" She hollered.

He leaned in close and whispered, "No more drugs in my bar, do you understand?"

She laughed, and as she threw her head back, the stool wobbled and she fell hard onto the polished wooden floor, "Is that why he left? Jesus."

Leo jumped the bar and pulled her back upright and led her by her arm to the corner of the room, next to where the cutlery and plates were stacked. "Sit here and don't move." Before she could blink, he was back and placed a pint of water in front of her, "Drink this, all of it." He sat down having ordered one of the others to cover the bar.

"You, don't know," she slurred.

"Keep drinking," he pushed the water back towards her. His dismissal infuriated her.

"I said, YOU DON'T KNOW…"

"Listen, is there someone I can call, where are you staying?"

"Shush, shush," she put her finger to her lips, "listen, you need to listen…your girlfriend was my dad's whore." She nodded and smiled.

"What are you talking about?"

"Tate, right? Your girlfriend? Well, she was my dad's whore." She watched as his face drained in colour, and her tummy somersaulted with the power she wielded over him.

He stood up, and glanced around, then yanked her out of the door to the back of the bar and outside into the courtyard where empty crates were stacked. "You're hurting me you fucker."

"What the hell are you talking about?" She could see his mind putting things together, "You, it was you who graffitied the shop? What the fuck are you playing at?"

She shrugged her shoulders and as she vomited onto the floor, it peppered his legs. He clenched his teeth and pushed her down onto the floor, "Hey, don't touch me," she shouted in between retching, "Get your hands off me."

He disappeared and came back with a towel and water, he wiped his legs first and handed it to her, putting the water beside her. She looked up to the sky but it was spinning and so she lay down for a moment to stop it. She could hear him on the phone.

"Come now, something I need help with."

She imagined it was Tate, and that she would arrive soon. They were on to her...but she passed out before she could do anything about it.

TATE

Tate lent back in her chair and rubbed her tummy; she was full up. Usually she opted for tapas, but for some reason she chose the steak, and ate every mouthful.

"God, I cannot eat another thing."

"Not even a little bit of pudding? We could share?" Her mum loved a pudding.

"Seriously Mum, did you see the size of that steak I ate? No pudding for me."

"Well maybe a little dessert wine then, we could manage that couldn't we?"

Tate nodded, it was 9.30 and she should be heading off soon.

"You don't mind me leaving you and heading off to Miguel's? You can always come too?" It was an empty offer, and she hoped her mum would decline.

"I don't mind at all, I'm in the middle of a good book, so I'm going to settle on the terrace and enjoy a glass or two of wine. The perfect end to the evening for me."

Tate smiled, "Well, I will settle up and head off then, I could do with a walk to ease this steak down a bit."

"No dessert wine then?"

"Go on then, but I'll pay up and order them at the same time though, okay?"

"Thank you darling, but I'd like to treat you. It's lovely to see you doing so well out here, but I worry about you." Eileen waved and caught the waiter's eye, who rushed over.

"May we have two dessert wines and the bill please, how do you say it, is it La Cuenta?"

"Of course, two dessert wines and the bill, coming up," he nodded and dashed back to the bar.

"You don't need to worry about me mum, I'm good. Life's ok, I thought you may feel better about it all, now you've seen my home and the shop for yourself, and please let me get this?"

"No! This is my treat and I'm not arguing about it."

Tate sighed, "Okay, okay! I know when I can't win. Thank you."

The waiter placed a glass down in front of each of them, "Ladies, your drinks, and here is the bill."

"Great thanks," Tate smiled.

Eileen lifted her glass towards Tate, "To you. I'm so proud of you, it's lovely seeing you settled, but after everything that happened with Richard, I mean, is he still around, bothering you? I wondered if he may have been the one who had your shop graffitied? I know you said he turned out to be horrid..."

Tate reached across the table and grabbed her mum's hand, "You really don't need to worry. I promise. Richard is long gone. It was probably some druggies maybe or bored kids..." Tate hated lying to her mum, she had spent so long doing it, painting the happy life story, settled with 'Richard', (her made-up name for Bill.) Somehow, when they were in separate countries, the lying didn't feel so bad. She could convince herself that it was to protect her mum from the truth, yet now as she sat facing her, looking into her eyes, guilt almost prevented her from speaking. It was still for her mum's good, to keep her from the truth. Imagine if she were to discover the real story. What good would that do anyway?

Her life had moved on, she was settled and happy and if she could resolve this   issue with Ellie, all really would be well, regardless of what happened with Leo.

"Well, okay, but you have to understand, that as your mum, I will always worry about you. That's just how it goes. I do feel better knowing that you have Irena here, and maybe now Leo…"

"It's early days."

"Uh-huh, but he is lovely," Eileen smiled and nodded.

"Shall I come back with you? Keep you company?" Guilt pecked away at her.

"Absolutely not! I am looking forward to my own company I told you! Go, finish up your drink, and get gone," she sipped her wine. "It's so delicious, you are lucky this is a local delicacy and so reasonably priced! I need to take some home with me, although I wonder if it will taste the same beneath the cloudy Southampton sky!"

"Probably not! Thanks for dinner mum," she stood and kissed her cheek, "love you. See you later."

Tate left the restaurant, hoping she had done enough to convince her mum that all was well.   Maybe she should be going back with her, rather than heading over to see Leo. But she couldn't avoid him forever, and she didn't want to, things were promising with him. No, she needed to deal with this head on, and pull up her big girl's pants. She had faced worse. Hopefully this was simply a blip, a silly young girl was not going to mess with *her* life.

She pulled her cardigan over her shoulders and strode down past the church tower as it chimed 10. The square was busy, and groups of people spilled out from the tables and bars and were dancing to music being played by a band. She stopped for a moment. Mauricio's voice belted out over a music system, and he strutted around with his guitar. The gaggle of girls pointing and trying to catch his attention tickled her, and her face erupted into a smile. That one would never change.

Miguel's was tucked away down a side street and was rammed with people, so she fought her way through on tip toe, looking for Leo, who she expected to be behind the bar. The faces serving weren't the usual staff and they were struggling to cope with the six deep queue. She scanned the room, but there was no sign of him. She pushed through to the back and found a space big enough to pull out her phone and text him. WHERE ARE YOU? X

He texted back immediately, COME OUT THE BACK THROUGH THE STAFF ONLY DOOR

Puzzled, Tate proceeded outside and saw the back of Irena's head. Her curls bounced as she spoke, and her bangles jingled with every gesticulation. Someone was slumped on the ground.

"We need to talk," Leo said immediately on spotting her.

Tate's stomach churned and she instantly regretted the huge dinner, "Okay, what's going on, IRENA?"

Irena stood to the side and Tate got a clear view of the slumped figure, it was Ellie.

77

"Oh finally, here she is. Took her time, didn't she?" Ellie slurred and waved her hands.

"Shut up." Irena was clearly at her limit, "I have heard enough from your foul mouth."

"Ellie, what are you doing?" Tate crouched down next to her.

"So, you do know her then?" Leo asked.

Tate nodded, "Yes I was going to talk to you tonight."

"Don't speak in front of her." Irena turned to Tate, "Don't say another thing in her earshot, she is poisonous."

"Like I haven't heard that before," Ellie tried to sit up but slumped back down. Her matted hair was tangled with vomit and dried blood.

Leo moved Tate to the far side of the courtyard, "we do need a conversation, yes. In fact, looking at how my evening has gone, that's the least you owe me. But right now, we need to sort this out. She's been doing drugs in my toilets and is off her head."

Tate nodded and rubbed his arm, wishing she had already come clean about everything with him. He shrugged her off. "Did she fall over?" Tate pointed to the deep welt on her scalp.

"No that's not a fresh cut, she already had that. But I don't want this in here, in my bar. I can't have drugs around, taken years to build up the bar's reputation, and I'm not having it."

Tate knew he was pissed off about the drugs, and so he should be, but the anger was more aimed at her, and whatever Ellie had said to him.

"It seems she damaged your shop too, apparently. Has some axe to grind with you, so are we calling the police?"

Tate shook her head, "Look at the state of her, what good are the police going to do? No police."

"She needs a lesson taught; the police are exactly what she needs." Leo's red face was almost unrecognisable to Tate.

"No Leo, I don't want police involved."

Irena joined them, "Listen Leo, Tate is right, no police. She is clearly under the influence of more than drugs and alcohol, someone is pulling her strings. Whatever her motive, she needs help."

"I don't need your help! I don't need anything from you. Apart from my money – you can give me that, yeh, give me the money." Ellie's slurred words carried on the air and Leo looked towards Tate and then Irena.

"What money? What's this about?" His voice was low, and he was doing his best to stay calm, but his fists were clenched into tight balls. "Actually, get her out of here. There's too many people around, take her the back way." He was already unlocking the gate.

"Up you get," Tate pulled Ellie to her feet, and was wondering where to take her.

"Don't worry, I've got someone waiting for me, you'll see, right around that corner."

Tate and Irena exchanged glances and shrugged as they led her through the gate. Tate turned to speak to Leo, but the gate was closed and locked behind them.

"Let's take her home to yours?"

"No, you heard her, she has someone waiting. Who is waiting for you?" Irena shook Ellies shoulders.

"My taxi, my taxi is waiting…round here…" She staggered up the cobbled hill and pointed. Tate recognised it as the car which picked her up from their viewpoint meeting.

"Come back with us Ellie, we will look after you," Tate pleaded.

But Ellie pushed her away and sped her stagger up towards the car, "Get the fuck away from me…I want my money, just give it back." She yelled.

"Leave her Tate," Irena grabbed her hand and they watched as Ellie clambered into the car, which pulled away up the road and out of sight.

"We should have taken her home, she needs help. We allowed her to go back to Tony or whoever is fucking her up."

"She would have run away as soon as she was able, she doesn't want help, she wants to ruin you."

"She is doing a pretty good job of it, looking at Leo's face earlier."

"What did you expect him to look like? Get real...Listen, he's a nice guy. He's been around the block a few times; he understands how things go. But he hates lies, you need to be honest with him. The whole truth."

Tate winced, "The whole truth is messy. Maybe too messy for him. But you are right, he deserves an explanation, what-ever the outcome."

Irena nodded and squeezed her hand, "Go back, reach out to him, that's all you can do." They wove through the streets back to the front of the bar. "I'm going home, my headache will not leave me today. Good luck."

Tate nodded, "Feel better, and Irena, I do listen."

Irena smiled and wearily walked off towards home.

Tate stood amongst the throng of people and waited her turn to be served. "Straight Jack please with ice," Leo nodded and poured her a large, refusing her offer of payment. He continued serving but she stood firm and sipped her drink watching him navigate the bar like a pro. She would be gutted if this was the end, but most blokes would run for the hills. She hoped the connection which she had felt with him, was enough to give her a chance. After a few minutes, Leo leaned in and beckoned her nearer with his finger.

"Once this lot dies down, I will be free and then we can talk." He plonked another jack on the bar in front of her and cleared enough space for her to sit on the stool, so he could keep an eye on her she supposed.

Tate wondered where Ellie had gone and what she was doing. All she could think of was the world she had once fallen into, and to what lows she stooped. She hadn't succumbed to the drugs, but if she had she doubted she would still be around. Tony's lot threw drugs around like sweets, knowing that it gave them the upper hand. Reel them in, and watch them scratch around for the white stuff, she had seen that a thousand times before. Maybe she should contact Ellies mum? But realistically what could she do? A firm elbow from a drunken reveller knocked her drink over her lap and she gasped and jumped down from the stool.

"Sorry, sorry," he said, "Let me help you," his eyes widened and focussed in on her sodden, low-cut shirt. He grabbed a napkin and patted at her breasts as though he was trying to soak up the spillage.

"It's fine, please leave it." Tate pushed his grabby hands away.

"Hey, cut it out, or leave," Leo warned him, and he immediately raised his hands in defeat and   shuffled away into the crowd. "Take this and wait for me at home, I'll be there as soon as I can." Leo pressed his key into Tate's hand and continued serving, so she pushed back outside into the cooler night air and wandered up the street. The sky was peppered with stars, and it look magical. She sighed. He must be willing to listen, he must want to hear her truth. But could he stomach it?

Leo's house, it was similar in lay out to hers, but much more organised and less cluttered. She closed the shutters and peeled off her soggy clothes which she took to the sink to soak in soapy water. His kitchen was immaculate, and nothing clogged up the worktops, everything seemed to have a place. She headed upstairs to the lounge and flicked on a dim corner lamp. A large armchair sat next to it, and she settled on it, beneath a cream blanket, which lay folded over the arm. From there she   continued to size up the surroundings.

There were a few photographs up on the wall, but mainly of mountains and forests, which had been enlarged and printed in black and white. They looked dramatic. His coffee table was clear except for his running watch and his earphones. Neat logs were stacked next to the open fire, ready for more chillier winter evenings. His clock ticked loudly, and the steady rhythm made her eyes heavy, and when sleep came, it was Leos face she saw.

ELLIE

She stopped the car three times, surely, she had nothing left inside to vomit. It was only bile and tasted like poison. If she ever needed the driver to offer her a cold water, like that very first day, it was then, but his disdain for her was evident. "You can clean up and pay for any mess you make," he reminded her on the final stop as she heaved and choked onto the dusty mountain road.

Ellie searched her bag for a chewing gum, but the packet was empty, "Please don't say the boss needs to see me tonight? I really can't."

The driver said nothing. Ellie crossed her fingers. She leant back onto the leather head rest and closed her eyes, she could not face Tony, not with spew splattered all over. He wouldn't approve. She quickly glanced outside and sighed with relief; the car was heading to her apartment.

Once behind her locked door, she slid to the floor and cried. Her tears were muddled, confusing, self-pitying. Some were for how rough she felt, and some were finally for her dad. She looked around through her watery eyes, and realised in two weeks, she hadn't even unpacked her case. Her bed was unmade, her fridge empty and the apartment cold and sad. She opened the patio doors and stood looking out towards the moonlit mountains. The streets were still noisy below and life sounded fun for the revellers wandering home. Why was hers so dark now? She should have left the past firmly alone. But why should Tate enjoy the money which was so rightfully hers?

She crawled towards the bathroom and switched on the shower, which she climbed into fully clothed. The steaming water cascaded over her and mingled with her self-pitying tears. Tears were not her style, and yet this trip was messing with her. She was unrecognisable even to herself. She peeled off her clothing and threw them into the bath and scrubbed at her body. Where was her fight gone, her energy, her courage? She felt empty and lost. A guttural scream echoed around her bathroom, and she stamped her feet and tensed her arms into clenched fists. Her heart raced and adrenaline flooded her body. She was in deep, but she wasn't going to give up.

She needed to dig deeper, to fight harder and to reach the end goal – making Tate pay. Pay for her dad's death and for the money she stole. Tony was the key to that, she needed him to achieve this. Then she could go home, and never return. Until then, she needed to up her game. Her mouth twisted into a smile, at least she brought Leo's attention to Tate's past, and the whole town saw her message on the shop. Her cage had certainly been rattled, and her cosy little life shaken up.

Tony's motive remained unclear. Why after all this time, was he focussing his attention on Tate and so eager to help her? Why hadn't he acted earlier? The knot in her stomach returned when she thought about what Tony was capable of. Hopefully, if she followed his instructions, they could both get what they wanted. She pushed the feelings of unease away and ran her fingers across the welt on her head, it was healing but still sore.

After her shower Ellie headed to the tapas bar two buildings along, hoping they would still serve food. She remained in sight of the car, parked permanently, watching.

"Can I have one of each of the top dishes please, and some bread and a beer?" Her growling   stomach made her realise how little she was eating lately, and she was suddenly ravenous. Almost immediately the tapas dishes were silently placed before her together with a cold beer. "Gracias," she smiled at the lady who nodded in return. The bar was dated but clean and a few locals sat   chatting, with late night Spanish radio playing low in the background.

"Here, you look like you need feeding up," the lady placed a plate with two churros and a chocolate dip in front of her, "free, for you." She spoke in broken English and squeezed her hand. Ellie's eyes filled with tears at the kindness offered, and she tucked into the food, feeling the stress and tension slowly fade. It felt safe enough to relax and for the first time in ages, she dropped her guard and enjoyed the moment, with no immediate agenda except to feed her starving body. It was the most delicious meal she could ever recall eating, and when she had finished everything including the churros, she rubbed at her contented tummy.

Her phone beeped, and it was a relief to see her Mum, instead of Tony: **PLEASE LET ME KNOW YOU ARE OK? ITS TORTURE NOT KNOWING, AND I CAN'T SLEEP FOR WORRY. JUST A THUMBS UP WOULD DO? AT LEAST TO LET ME KNOW YOU'RE STILL ALIVE. LOVE YOU xx**

She sighed, the last thing she needed was her mum in panic mode, launching some search for her. So, she reluctantly sent a thumbs up emoji, hoping that would keep her at bay for a while.

Immediately her mum responded: **OH, THANK GOD YOU ARE OK. BEEN SO WORRIED. I WISH YOU WOULD COME HOME, I DON'T UNDERSTAND WHY YOU ARE OUT THERE, I AM SCARED YOU WILL RUN INTO PEOPLE FROM YOUR DAD'S PAST. BE CAREFUL. WE LOVE YOU ELLIE. Xx**

She could never be grateful, constantly wanted more from her. That always happened, if she sent any kind of lame response, her mum would issue a barrage of messages in return, desperate for her attention. That was not happening, so she clicked off her phone, determined to ignore any further messages that followed.

TATE

As she wiped the sleep from her eyes Leo's face came into focus, "Hi. Sorry, took much longer to get away then I planned."

He crouched next to her, with two glasses of red wine in his hand, "thought we may both need a drink to get through this." Tate sat up and stretched her legs as Leo put their glasses on the coffee table, "you can put this on too." He threw a t-shirt over. She pulled it over her head and inhaled his scent.

She reached for her wine and took a sip, "Thanks, what time is it?"

"Just after two," Leo sat on the floor opposite and wedged a cushion between his back and the sofa, "That was a crazy Wednesday night, not sure what that was about, I'm not complaining, but I could have done without the drama." He drank his wine, "I hate drama."

Tate sniffed hard, if he hated drama, this was all about to go very wrong. "I don't know where to start really."

"Who is Ellie to you?"

"She's my ex, my ex-bosses' daughter."

Leo's eyebrows arched, "Your ex-boss?"

Tate nodded. "Okay Leo, I don't know what Ellie has told you, or how many actual facts, she has. So, are you sure you want the full story? My version- the truth?" She knelt beside him and touched his cheek with the back of her forefinger. She stared into his eyes and hoped this wouldn't be the last time they were so close. "So, it started about 5 years ago, when I arrived in Spain. I was young and naïve, first time abroad alone. You know how that is, you see them all the time coming into your bar?"

Leo stared over the rim of his glass, "Right, and then?"

"I got a job in a bar down on the coast and met a bloke. Thought he was lovely, charmed me, we got serious quickly. Well, let me rephrase that, I got serious quickly. And before I knew it, we were   living together. Trouble was he owed a lot of money to some questionable people, and his habits, mainly gambling and drugs, meant the amount racked up daily. They came looking for him at our place one day, I was unlucky enough to be home…"

Tate guzzled her wine, and poured another, "I don't really like talking about this, it's a time I want to forget ever happened."

"I need to hear it," Leo stared, and she knew he would only be satisfied with the whole unpalatable truth.

"So, he wasn't in, I was. Next thing I knew I woke up in a villa, with three other girls. Basically, there to serve the 'associates.' One of the other girls slipped something into my drink the first time, said it would help. But it didn't," Tate shuddered. "No matter how many showers I took, I couldn't wipe him off me. After that, I felt as though there was no way back. I was damaged goods. The lunacy and danger of it all is that the longer you spent among those people, the more it seemed as though that was normal."

"And Ellies dad?"

"Bill."

"As in Bill, Tony and Paul?" He shook his head and sighed.

"Yes, you know of them already then. Well, he was one of the better ones in the sense he wasn't as brutal. He seemed to single me out. In some ways, he saved me, because I could have ended up in a much worse position, he warned me to keep my head down, do as I was told. Once I was beaten so badly, not by him. But as a warning to him. Anyway, to cut a long story short, I thought he cared for me, but looking back it was like he was grooming me. Manipulating me to service his needs. He tried to convince me to do a drug run, because he said his daughter, Ellie, was in danger. He told me he loved me, that we would be together. In my mind we would escape and set up a new life. But he was only stringing me along, using me. Luckily, at the last minute, I realised the truth. So, I stole his money. I emptied his safe."

Leo spluttered and red wine splashed his shirt, "What?"

"I stole all of it. And gave some away, to a deserving person who helped me many times. And then he was killed in a fire, I suspect Tony, one of the crazies, had some involvement, but the physicality of the crime was committed by Jose."

"You're talking about Caminos, aren't you?"

Tate nodded, "You were around then?"

"No, I knew of it before I left Spain. Everyone knew about Caminos, could never work out why they got away with so much shit. We all knew Jose had lost it, finally reached the end of the line, when it burnt down. Shame he never made good afterwards."

"He lit the match. Paul and Bill perished, but officially, no one was inside, and they simply   disappeared off the radar, no one seemed to care. But now, he is so fucked up, his marriage fell apart and he drunk his new bar dry. Poor Jose. I owed him a lot." Tate shrugged and shook her head, "Anyway with my part of the cash, I retrained as a florist and set up in business with Irena."

"Does Irena know all of this?"

"I wouldn't be here if it wasn't for her, she gave me the strength to leave, and offered me a home. Not once did she ever blame me for what Bill did to her."

"What did he do to her?"

"He beat her up, looking for me."

Leo's face flushed and the tiny veins in his forehead popped, "Fucking hell, if he wasn't dead I'd kill him." He stood up and paced the floor.

"I know this is a lot to take in, you're angry with me."

"Of course I'm fucking angry. What did you expect me to do, nod and make reassuring noises?" He emptied the bottle into his glass and turned to face her, "So Ellie is here because..."

"Well, I guess she worked out that I took some money from Bill. And maybe she thinks I killed him? It was her I met the other night, when you asked me where I had been, she told me that there was evidence somewhere, footage. Probably me at the safe? I don't know but she wants money, trouble is, I'm scared for her. Scared for who she is involved with."

"Tate, have you been tested, since you...?" Leo seemed unsure how to finish his sentence, "since you were a sex worker?"

She sucked in her breath and her wide eyes fought back tears. He asked in such a cold, matter of fact way. "Do you think I would have slept with you if I hadn't? I don't know what you think I am, but I didn't choose that life, and I didn't stay."

"You should have been honest from the start."

"Hmmm, how should I have phrased that? Leo, I am really attracted to you, I would like this to go somewhere, but hold on a minute, I was a sex worker, so can you sign this disclaimer and acknowledge this before we continue? Or maybe I could have walked you through my injury map, like here, on my head where my hair was ripped out? Or here if you look closely on my thigh, you can make out teeth marks."

The room was silent, except for the punctuated tick of the clock. Tate stood up.

"Where are you going? You can't do a runner because I haven't thrown my arms around you."

"You need space, to think about everything I just told you. None of it's easy to verbalise, and I don't even like thinking about it now."

He grabbed her hand, "I don't want you to leave."

She sighed and stared at the floor. The flashing memories of her attack physically shook her as she wrapped her arms around her body, "what are we going to do?"

"I don't know," he shrugged, "I don't know what to say."

He slumped onto the sofa and chewed his lip.

"Do you still want to be with me?" she whispered.

"My head is spinning, and I feel so fucking angry."

"I understand. I'm not the person you thought I was, I get it, really I do."

She dropped onto the sofa, next to him, and stared at a moth which was flying around the lamp. The ticking of the clock which earlier aided her sleep, sounded louder and irritating. She felt an urge to smash it to the floor.

"Listen, I have no answers for you, I can't fix any of what you have told me. But I'm not going   anywhere." He shuffled around to face her, "Let's sleep on it. I'm so tired I can't think straight. I'll clear my head in the morning with a run and we can see what tomorrow brings, that's all I can give you right now."

Tate followed him upstairs to his bedroom, her stomach tied in knots, fearful that this could be the end before they even got started. But he hadn't asked her to leave, so that was a good sign surely? She climbed in next to him, and he pulled her close. Her shivering soon ceased, she felt safe, despite the uncertainty, and silently begged him not to let her go.

"Have you thought about a fresh start? Like selling up?" Leo rolled over and gulped the pint of water beside his bed.

"This is my fresh start, the florist and my home. For the first time I'm settled, and can afford to live a decent life independently," Tate rolled over and leant on her elbow.

"I don't really understand then," he lay on his back, his hands up behind his head.

"Now I'm confused that you don't understand? Perhaps we are both exhausted and   misunderstanding?"

"I think you know exactly what I'm saying Tate. Your fresh start was created from *his* money. He will always lurk in your peripheral, it's no fresh start."

Tate's eyes pricked with tears, "Then you really don't understand." She rolled over and faced the wall.

93

"It's not always easy to hear the truth, and I do believe that deep down, you know what I'm saying is true. You are an intelligent woman, and you cannot tell me that these thoughts never crossed your mind?"

"I told you everything I suffered because of Bill. He owed me a better life, a chance at happiness. Bloody hell that was the very least he owed me. So no, I don't believe what you are saying, I think if anything, you don't like the thought of my past. But I can't change it, and this is me, making the best of a shit situation."

"Hey, this is coming from concern, and because I care for you. I love seeing you laugh and watching you grow your business. But everything that is happening to you now, it's because of that money. That connection. Surely you understand that?"

Tate sighed, "It's a price I'm willing to pay."

"So how are you going to appease Ellie. What if she really has evidence that you took the money? How are you going to pay her off?"

"I'm still thinking about that. I have twenty grand in the bank, I might have to give her that."

"Would she be happy to take that? I get the impression she won't rest until she sees you give it all up."

Tate yawned, "It has to be worth a try, perhaps I should offer her it sooner than later, it may   encourage her to pack up and get as far away from Tony as possible. I keep thinking about the welt on her head, and what he could have done to her. It honestly makes me shudder."

94

Leo pulled Tate back towards him, and spooned her, "We can figure this out together, if you let me help."

Tate squeezed his hand, but inner turmoil began to whirl, as she hoped he wasn't displaying traits of control. She didn't need him to rescue her financially, or otherwise.

ELLIE

For the first time, Ellie's head felt clear when she woke. She had eaten well in the past few days, Tony seemed to be letting her have some time off and she was trying a bit harder to keep herself together. She found a small complex of apartments nearby with a pool and decided she would use it. It would be easy to pretend to know someone or be staying there if she was questioned. So far not another soul had used it whilst she was there. The water gave her life. It seemed to be bringing back some of the old Ellie, and she felt revived.

She smiled at the fridge which contained some eggs and juice, water and fruit and felt accomplished, like a proper grown up. Her clothes were now neatly folded away, and it felt a bit more like a sanctuary. God knows she needed one. Her head was still a mess with the events which had swept her up into the eye of a storm. Her feet were only now touching the ground again, the first time since arriving in Spain. The drugs were a problem, weakened everything about her and she felt like a puppet being manipulated at the thought, sight or promise of them.

She waved as she passed the tapas bar with the kind 'churros' lady and continued along the street, her straw bag on her shoulder with her beach towel. The sun was already beating relentlessly and sweat beaded her tanned skin. The old guy with the newspaper -stand, handed her a paper and refused payment. She stopped for a moment and wondered why, but he was busy serving a Spanish family who were immediately deep in animated conversation. She shrugged and put it into her bag.

The pool was surrounded all sides with palms and well main-tained, lush green gardens. Around the edge of these sat the terraced houses. Iron railings enclosed the pool, and as Ellie opened the gate, she sighed with relief to once again have the space to herself. A distant radio played a Spanish morning show, and a washing machine rumbled from some-where. Her favourite lounger was beneath the shade of a parasol near the edge of the compound, and it gave her a clear view of   approaching people, and time to prepare her justification for being there. As she pulled out and shook her towel, the newspaper fell onto the lounger and the face on the front page caught her eye.

She slumped down and lifted the paper to read. It was the guy who had been at her apartment, who used to run Caminos, Jose. He was dead. Her eyes tried to make sense of the information, but her poor Spanish hindered her. Her mind whirled. It reeked of Tony. He must have some connection. Jose had been to see her, in the last few weeks, would the

Police know this? Would her name come up? She dug into the side pocket of her bag and dabbed her finger in powder, before rubbing it into her gums. She needed to calm the fuck down. She was jumping to conclusions and couldn't even read the article. No, she would forge ahead with her day, and cool down in the water for now. Perhaps the kind lady in the tapas bar could help, she spoke English, al be it broken, but it was better than her own grasp of Spanish.

The water could not calm her. Even, gliding through, swimming underwater lengths, her mind refused to quieten, instead throwing questions around, which agitated her. Her throat constricted as her mind flashed back to her 'net incident' with Tony and she swam to the side and climbed out. Her eyes scanned the surrounding area, as she dabbed the towel all over, was she still being watched? The car hadn't been parked outside for a few days...there appeared to be no one, (well no one obvious at least), but she was surrounded by houses and could not see inside them, so potentially he could have eyes on her. As she perched on the edge of the lounger, fully exposed to the sun to dry, her senses pricked like a rash erupting across her body. A shiver ran down her spine as she threw over her clothes onto her still damp body and packed away her things. Her brisk walk erupted into a run, and she flung open the gate and onto the road back towards the relative safety of the Tapas bar. Out of the corner of her eye, she glimpsed the car parked over from her apartment and suddenly her fatigue returned. If only she wasn't so stubborn, why didn't she leave in the last quiet few days? Why could she not back down and go home?

"Hola!" She fake-smiled on entering the bar, and sat at a table further inside, away from the   exposure of the front. The lady automatically brought over a coffee and pastry.

This time Ellies smile wasn't fake, "Gracias."

"How are you today? Good swim?"

"Yes, I'm okay, thanks and you?"

"Yes and no."

"Ooh, I know exactly what you mean. That sums my life up. Can you help me? My Spanish is crap, and I want to know what this says?" Ellie pulled out the newspaper and placed it on the table in front of them.

The lady made the sign of the cross and muttered something indistinguishable. "This is why I'm not so good," Her flat hand pointed repeatedly towards the picture. "Jose was found dead. It is so sad."

"Does it say what happened to him?"

"Car crash, he was drunk."

Ellie's shoulders relaxed, perhaps it was an accident after all. "I didn't mean to upset you," she squeezed the kind lady's hand and sipped her coffee.

The lady sat down opposite Ellie and leaned in close, "Jose hadn't driven for years. Never went   anywhere, no need to drive. Sold his car when the money ran out, just before the bar closed." Her eyes widened and her head nodded.

The boarded-up windows, and grubby 'Bar Jose' sign popped into Ellie's mind. It was symbolic of the world from where she found herself entangled. "Are you trying to say, you don't believe it?"

She nodded again, "It is too strange. Why would he steal a car and drive it over the edge of a   mountain? Surely, he would have drunk himself to death, or overdose even, if he wanted to kill   himself?"

"He was heading that way, from what I saw of him," she didn't want to reveal his recent, late-night visit, so chose her wording carefully.

"Maybe he wasn't doing it quick enough for someone. I mean, he was penniless, so he must have been getting help from somewhere, how else was he always full of alcohol? His wife leaving him, was the beginning of the end, she gave him so many chances to get away from," she lowered her voice to a whisper, "them."

Ellie leaned in close, "Do you think maybe he knew some-thing?"

"He knew too much, but it must have been something big, something more recent, otherwise they wouldn't have left him alone all this time..." She stood and rubbed her hands together, "I must get on. You be good, and it is nice to see you looking like you are taking more care of yourself. Much prettier."

Ellie smiled and waved. She was right. This had Tony written all over it. But what could he know? What if it was something about her dad, and her opportunity to find out was gone the moment she threw him out of her apartment?

The car still sat along the road. In the beginning, she thought it was funny, and laughed about how conspicuous it was. Now she realised that was the intention. They were not trying to hide it, they wanted her to feel intimidated and to know that they were watching her. She wasn't laughing about it anymore. Anytime soon her phone would go, and Tony would be issuing her orders again. She hoped she could avoid a similar fate to Jose. If she could hold her nerve, and keep her mouth in check, maybe this would all be over soon.

She pulled out her cigarettes from the bottom of her handbag and selected the least battered from the packet. Before she could rummage for her lighter, a flame appeared, and her head jerked. It was Leo, Tate's boyfriend. "Thanks, I take it this is no co-incidence? I mean, you are looking for me, right?"

Leo slipped the lighter into the pocket of his shorts, and nodded, "Let's have a walk shall we."

"Do I have a choice? I could scream…"

"Not your style. You may want to hear what I have to say."

"Okay Leo, you have my attention, so let's go. I want to let you know that I am being watched, so don't try anything."

Leo raised his eyebrows and looked around, fixing on the direction where her eyes rested. He nodded. "I want to talk to you, that's all."

Ellie followed his lead and they headed towards the park in silence. She finished her cigarette and immediately lit another.

"Chain smoking? Bit young for that?"

"Don't patronise me, what do you want anyway?"

Leo sat down on a nearby bench beneath a shady tree, and the cicadas above immediately silenced. Ellie stood facing him, drawing deep lung-fulls of smoke and purposely blowing it towards his face.

He laughed, "Oh that's so intimidating."

She scowled and stubbed out the butt with her foot. "Get on with it."

"You want your money, am I right?"

"MY money, your bitch of a girlfriend stole from my dad."

"That's why you are causing all this trouble for her? I want it to stop."

"Hey, you don't give me orders…"

"If you want your money, then it ALL needs to stop Ellie."

"Hmm," she slumped down next to him and chewed her nail. "It's not as simple as that. I told you I'm being followed. There are other people involved."

"I'm listening," Leo turned his body and leaned in towards her.

"That's all I can say, but I do want my money. Are you saying you can get me it? And If I leave her alone, that's it? What about my dad? What about revenging his death?"

"So, let me get this straight, you want to find out what happened to your dad? And you want your money?"

She nodded, "Finally, the penny drops."

"Well, I can help you with both. The money and the details of the fire. But I need a week or two."

"Really? Is this some bluff to stop me picking on your whore of a girlfriend?"

Leo winced, "Stop using that word or the deals off."

"I haven't agreed to any deal yet, I need time to think about this, how can I trust you?"

Leo sighed, "I don't care if you trust me or not. Sounds like you are in deeper than you know, and I don't want Tate involved – if giving you what you need, stops her life being screwed up, then it's worth every penny."

"She must be amazing in bed. I mean for you to care this much," Ellie smirked.

Leo stood up, "I've nothing else to say. The offer is there, I will start sorting my end of the bargain. You know where to find me. Oh, but don't come to Miguel's, your barred. You'll have to phone; you can find the number."

Ellies face dropped, "Fuck you." Her words echoed around her head as he walked away. Who did he think he was? Her face flushed red, and her fists clenched. She scrabbled in her bag and pulled out her squashed cigarettes, only one was intact. She frantically lit it and breathed in deep. Smoke billowed from her nose like a chimney. As her breaths calmed, she played over the information in her head. Maybe this was a better deal. She could get her money, find out what happened to her dad, and slip away quietly back to the UK, away from Tony. She needed to hold her nerve and do as she was told.

Her phone beeped and she jumped from her deep, racing thoughts. It was Tony. Co-incidence or did he already know about Leo? She ignored it and stood up, heading deeper into the park, further away from the prying eyes of the car. The phone continued to ring.

"Tony?"

"I told you to pick up when I ring," his voice was firm, but quiet.

"Sorry, I was on the loo," she smiled at her ingenuity.

"There are no loos in the park, what did lover boy want?"

Ellie gulped, and her face turned ashen, she spun around to see who could be watching her, but there was only a mum with her son walking a beagle.

"I'm waiting, I don't like being kept waiting," Tony's voice raised.

"He warned me away from Tate, told me to stop harassing her."

"That's all?"

"Yes, I told him to fuck off."

"That bitch is getting what she deserves, you are doing what your dad would want by rattling her cage. And soon, I will give you what you want. One more thing I need from you. But not now. I'll be in touch and make sure you answer straight away next time."

TATE

Tate picked up the pile of mail from her countertop, unable to put them off another day. They had accumulated over the previous few weeks and the longer she left them, the heavier they weighed on her conscience. She sidled through to Irena's, balancing two coffees in her hand, "Here, finished for the day unless I get some walk-ins."

"Thanks, pretty quiet day in here too."

Tate sifted through the pile of bills and stopped, curiously eyeing up the handwritten envelope with TATE written on the front.

"So, Leo took the truth ok, I mean you are still together?" Irena sipped her hot coffee and perched against a glass display cabinet full of colourful treasures.

"Jesus, it was awful. How I even found the words to say...he seemed to have accepted my past, in one way. But he is concerned about my finances and how my new life was 'funded'."

"Sounds sensible to me, I mean we have to think about what to do if we need to give Ellie money? It isn't clear if there is footage, although I thought Maria took care of that."

Tate nodded and sipped her coffee. "It's probably a bluff, and with no evidence, I'm not rushing to pay her a single penny...but he is riled up and feels like my past is still with us."

"He has a point," Irena shrugged.

"My mum can never know about any of this. It would kill her."

"It's such a shame she arrived at the same time as Ellie, I feel bad."

"You were trying to do a nice thing for me, and it's lovely having her here, but...I need her gone, for her own sake." Tate gnawed at her fingernail, "Convincing her of that, well..."

"Can't you say that Leo wants to take you away? She loves Leo..."

"Hmm, I need to think about it, and get her gone. The further away the better, I am living on eggshells and scared every time she goes out the door, in case she 'runs into' Ellie."

"I could have a quiet word, make her think it is her own idea?"

Tate hugged Irena tight, "What would I do without you?" and kissed her cheek.

"You would be screwed without me. It's true." She shrugged and sat down. "Here, use this." Irena handed an ornate gold letter opener, "new stock, call it research."

Tate smiled, "Fancy, I usually just rip them." She smiled and sliced open the envelope, pulling out the letter, which was neatly folded.

Tate,

This is long overdue and for that I am sorry.

I ruined everything. Lost my wife, my livelihood, my self-respect. All I had left was drink, so I hope you can understand why this became my sole reason for living. But it is not enough anymore. I don't want to live; I cannot live with the guilt. I saw things I should never have seen; you know that. But killing them in that fire, they have haunted me...

You need to know that Ellie is in danger, Tony is going to kill her. I cannot help her; I cannot get near her. You can, you know about Tony's house, you are the only one. You must or you too will be haunted by someone who's death you could have prevented.

I will always be grateful for the money, the belief you once had in me.

Goodbye

Jose

"What is it Tate?" Irena stood and snatched the letter from her paled friend's hand. "Shit. The trouble that girl brings to our door, it's almost as bad as when Bill was around. Tate your mum needs to be gone...and we need to work out what the hell we are going to do about this."

"I wouldn't be surprised if Leo doesn't run for the hills, I mean how much baggage can one woman have? He's already exasperated with it all, I know it."

"Where's your mum? We need to speed up her departure. Call her, tell her to come to the shop and leave the rest to me."

"Really? Okay. Should I go speak to Leo? I mean, tell him about this."

"Yes, it will only make him angrier if we keep it from him," Irena headed towards the buckets and blooms in the floristry part of the shop.

"I'll lock the shop up and head over to Miguel's, then." Dread weighed Tate down and she slowly followed Irena.

"No, you go, I will lock up," She pushed Tate away.

Tate turned towards the door, and then reversed and hugged Irena, "Thanks for always having my back."

"Always, but go now, stop stalling, let's get your mum on a flight tonight."

Tate messaged her mum: **GO TO IRENAS ASAP. DON'T WORRY, ALL OK. XX** and headed out of the shop into the heat of the sun, pulling her paper fan from her bag and wafting her face, the square was empty, and the bar owners congregated with coffee and a cigarette, relishing the moment of calm.

Miguel's was quiet too, as the church clock rang out the mid-day bells. Two local builders, sat in their grubby overalls chatting, and supped coffee. In the far corner, a mother sat discreetly feeding her new-born, whilst scrolling on her phone.

"Leo around?" Tate asked the waiter who busily polished glasses from the dishwasher.

"Out the back," he flicked his head towards the 'STAFF ONLY' door and continued his work.

Tate's phone beeped: **OKAY DARLING, ON MY WAY. X** Her unsuspecting mum would hopefully take the bait and be one less thing to worry about.

"Hey, you look busy," Tate pushed through the office door, and loomed above Leo.

Leo lay down a pile of paperwork and smiled, "Great, I need a valid reason to stop this and grab a coffee." He pulled Tate in close and kissed her lips, "Mmmm." He nuzzled her neck and trailed his lips down to her shoulder.

"Hey, I thought coffee really meant coffee," but she didn't mind and enjoyed his affection, and was a little relieved that he was still feeling it towards her.

"It does, and this is my place of work. So, let's be professional shall we. Coffee it is."

"Can I just have a water? I'm so hot." Tate turned towards the door.

Leo grabbed her hand and pulled her back into his arms, "Give me one more minute?" He squeezed her tight and inhaled her scent, she felt warm and safe, but knew that in a moment, this mood would be broken, like a shattered mirror bringing with it bad luck. "I've been worried about us," he said, "It's all getting a bit..." he broke off and pushed his lips to hers, firmly, his eyes closed. "We are good, aren't we?" He kissed her again, but she pulled back and frowned.

"Right, your right. Enough, let's get those drinks and find somewhere to sit."

"I could do with somewhere private, not in the bar?"

Leo raised his eyebrows, "Oh God. What's happened now? Why do I feel this unexpected little smooch, is about to turn sinister?"

Tate wrinkled her nose and pinched her lips. They felt dry so she dug inside her bag for a lip balm.

"Stay here then, I'll grab our drinks, back in a mo.," He darted out of the door.

Tate paced the room; it was the first time she had been inside his office and was surprised that it was a little messy. His desk was covered in paperwork, and she leaned over to glimpse what it all was. Expecting invoicing and VAT returns, she gasped to see they were all related to personal assets and valuations. Maybe he was selling up? Planning to leave after all. Her pulse raced; her conflicting emotions increased her hot flush. He couldn't leave now. What was all that kissing about, if he wasn't keen on her? Irena would have warned her if he was a player, he seemed genuine. She glanced out of the window, where a young woman was hanging out washing on an overhead line. Her chubby toddler proudly passed up the pegs to her, it was an idyllic picture. Why couldn't she have that, a normal family life, where thugs and gangsters didn't lurk.

A thought crept into her mind: maybe this was about what he suggested in bed, that she should give Ellie her money. That she should sell up- the shop, her home… Her head swam.

His footsteps got louder so she quickly dropped into the chair, not wishing him to think she may have snooped at his private information.

"Here we go. Although I did wonder if I should have opted for something stronger?" He handed her a glass of water half filled with ice, and a straw. "I thought the ice may help cool you down quicker," he said and perched on the edge of his desk, sipping and waiting for her to begin. His chin was stubbly, and his tortoise-shell glasses made his chiselled features more prominent, and a little nerdy in the shadowy light of the room. Her stomach somersaulted.

"So, I just found this in amongst my mail," she slid the letter from her bag and held it out.

Leo said nothing, but plucked it from her hand, unfolded it and read the words. He inhaled a deep breath, "for fucks sake."

"Yes," Tate answered.

"Is this all ever going to end? It's one thing after another? Fucking Tony," he folded it back up and threw it on his desk.

"I should take it to the Police, right? I mean it's practically a suicide note."

Leo shook his head and walked around his untidy desk to his chair. He shuffled together the paperwork into a neat pile and moved it to one side. "How do we know this was written by Jose?"

"What?"

"Exactly what I said. How do you know this was written by Jose? When did you last see Jose in any fit state to write anything? He didn't even know his own name most of the time, in the last few months. This is Tony." Leo removed his glasses and rubbed his eyes.

"What purpose would he have, to write this? To make it look like suicide when the whole town is whispering that someone staged it?"

"Maybe. But, more likely to lure you in."

"Oh, that's ridiculous, if Tony had an issue with me, then I would have been dead years back. Why now?"

Leo sighed and tapped his fingers on the table, "True."

"Perhaps it was Jose, and he really did want to say sorry to me, to help in one final way to make things ok."

"Even after everything, EVERYTHING you have been through, you still believe there is some good in all these people. Jose may have patched you up, he may have offered you words of comfort, but he stayed for years behind that bar, knowing everything he knew, seeing everything he saw. Don't be too quick to feel sorry for him, he was complicit in doing nothing. I have no sympathy for him. Karma is, as they say, a bitch." His narrowed eyes fixed on Tate.

Tate chewed her cheek and attempted to process his words, maybe he was right?

"I need to tell you something," Leo shuffled in his chair, "Don't be angry, but I went to meet Ellie."

"What?" Tate gasped.

"I offered her money and the truth about her dad, if she leaves you alone."

"You did what? Who's money? WHAT MONEY? WHAT TRUTH?" Tate stood, and anger seeped through her veins and out of her mouth as she shouted.

Leo rose to his feet, "Stop shouting at me. Someone had to take control of this situation. I was worried to broach the subject with you, but now, well now I know it was the right thing to do…I mean what next, is Tony about to burst in? Will his cronies murder you in your sleep, or me come to think of it!"

"How fucking dare you? You think because of my past, I owe you? I must make up for what I did before I even met you, like wiping away the life I have built on the money I believe was owed to me for what I went through? Or are you only scared, for yourself. Can't have them mess up your precious bar, god forbid anyone steps out of line," Tate knew she was out of control and gasped for air. "Fuck you, you have no clue."

"I see. I see now, how you feel. Is that what you really think of me? That little of me? You need to leave now, before any more is said," his arm pointed towards the door.

"Oh, you don't need to kick me out, I'm going. I don't need a Prince Charming to rescue me. I don't need you to sort out my life thanks." She snatched the letter from his desk and stormed out, slamming the office door hard behind her. She shook, and her body coiled tight, as she searched outside for someone smoking whom she could cadge a cigarette from. There was no-one, and she stormed towards the tobacconist and bought a packet, the first since Bill.

ELLIE

"Welcome, to your new home, please come in and put your stuff down. The girls will see to it. Drink?"

Ellie sighed and nodded, "vodka please."

"Not in a cocktail mood, no?" Tony clapped his hands, and the girls ran in, "Vodka for our guest and usual for me, oh and take care of Ellie's things please, put them in her room, will you? I thought she could have the guest suite overlooking the pool. She is a fan of the pool, and hopefully will get a chance to enjoy some time in there whilst she stays with us." His chatter was functional, and no reply was expected.

"What a warm welcome, thank you," she knew that she must keep her mouth in check, and play his game, just for a while longer.

In typical Tony style, he messaged Ellie and gave her one hour to pack up her things, before a knock on her door, to collect her. It was her usual driver of course, who had never got over their first meeting and the 'damage' she inflicted on him. Shame, because she would like to have seen what was on offer beneath his shirt and tie. You couldn't help but notice the cotton straining over his biceps, and he can only have been in his late twenties. For a moment, she hoped to see a glint of interest in his eye, but as usual, he stared coldly, and acted more of a prison guard transporting her, than an escort. She struggled to carry her bags down the stairs, as he sauntered down, smoking a cigarette and taking it easy. She scowled at the thought.

She only managed a garbled message to Leo, explaining that she was interested in their deal after all, but her time was almost up, as Tony was having her collected. He never got back to her, and it was too late now, she would have to play along with Tony.

"I want you to feel comfortable and at home whilst you are here, of course. Let's start with some of this shall we?" He opened the lid of the wooden box and pulled out a small bag which he began to cut and line up.

Ellie sidled over and smiled, "Sure, thanks."

"Subdued? So out of character. You'll soon get used to your new place, here, take the edge off."

They snorted the powder and settled on the oversized sofa with their drinks. It was comfortable and enveloping, but she felt vulnerable and small. Her head swam. Why did he need her here? What was his plan?

"I expect you're wondering why I summoned you here. Why I need you to stay?"

Ellie shuddered, could he read her mind?

"Well, it's simple, I felt bad. Figured you should get to spend some time here, enjoying the facilities. As you know I have a wonderful pool, and a bubbling hot tub, and thinking of you in that tiny apartment with no real outside space. What would your dad think if I didn't let you have some enjoyment?"

Ellie relaxed a little. Maybe she could afford to chill until his final plan was executed. Then leave with her money, "To be honest that sounds lush."

Tony smiled, "Good. Good."

"Can I have a swim in a minute?"

"Sure you can, make sure you grab a towel from the basket down there and let me show you to your room first, but take it easy, relax, all in good time, enjoy your drink."

Tate waved her mum through the gates at the airport, and relief washed over her. It was two-fold, firstly that she would be safe, but also that she was less likely to be privy to any information she didn't want her finding out. It was all too messy. Irena worked her magic like a pro, convincing her mum that she should allow Leo and her time together, and that she may soon hear wedding bells and could come back over to plan the wedding. Huh, if only she knew the truth. Leo was as controlling as Bill in some ways. Playing her like a puppet, going behind her back and trying to organise her finances. She didn't need any man to save her.

"Hey, it's me, can you hear me? Not great signal at the airport. I'm on my way, driving home now, about an hour probably."

"Drive safe Chica. What the hell has happened with Leo?"

"Can we talk later; I'm so stressed out. I will come to you, yes?"

"Okay, I'll throw some food together."

"Great."

Irena would be on Leo's side. Why did she always take their side? That wasn't strictly true, she hated Bill from the start, and he NEVER did anything right in her eyes. It used to drive Tate mad, but look how that turned out, she was right all along. Maybe she would listen to her side of things and then she would understand that Leo was being controlling. She turned up the radio, and steadily drove along the motorway before turning off up the winding mountainous terrain. When she first arrived, the roads filled her with terror, and she always shut her eyes rather than risk looking over the edge. Now she drove them with ease, knowing every twist and turn, even in the dark with only moonlight to guide her. The sky was clear, and the stars, like pin pricks of bright light in a blackout.

Would life ever be normal again? Would someone always be lurking in the shadow to steal her   happiness, or the breath from her lungs? Whatever Leo's views on the letter, she knew she needed to help Ellie. Ellie was only a young kid, caught up in a treacherous world that she didn't understand. Tate had the advantage of knowing the layout of Tony's place, and if she could blag her way in one of the secret exits Tony created for emergencies, she could remove Ellie from Tony's clutches.   Maybe she would be so grateful, that she would accept the twenty grand, and life could return to normal.

Tomorrow, she would feign sickness, not open the shop. Then she could sneak there, perhaps she should torch the damn place whilst there…finish it for good. The police were no use, they seemed to have some sort of 'distance agreement', and as Tony was 'laying low', they let him be. Irena could never know, because she would tie Tate to a chair, before letting her go there. Maybe, she was   going crazy, losing the plot, because if she spoke the words, verbalised her plan, she herself would be forced to admit, it was ridiculous. And yet, she knew that nothing would stop her.

The town was calm, she parked at home and walked to Irena's, avoiding the area of Miguel's. Her stomach rumbled and she realised she had nothing to eat since breakfast. As she arrived in the square, she could hear low music and the delicious aroma of garlic wafting from Irena's Juliet balcony. Her mouth watered in anticipation as she let herself in through the side door. "Only me, and I'm starving."

She took the stairs two at a time and threw her bag over the banister by the kitchen, "God I'm so hungry." She kissed Irena's cheek and moved out of her way, as she was busy dishing up the food.

"Good, I seem to have made enough to feed an army, go pour us a drink and sit at the table." Tate lifted the bottle of rioja, already opened to breathe, and poured a glass each. She gulped down hers and repoured before settling back in the chair and exhaling.

"Here," Irena dotted the dishes around the table, "Dig in, and there's more so have as much as you like."

Tate filled her plate and began to munch away, moaning with delight at the explosion of flavours.

"Wow. When did you last eat?" Irena sipped her wine and was still choosing her food when Tate began her second helping.

"This morning, suddenly I'm famished. It must be relief as well, that mum has gone now. I was more edgy than I realised maybe?"

"And Leo? You managed to screw that up already? Tate, he is a good one, not a snake like Bill, or brat like Mauricio, genuinely a good guy. Is that not enough for you?"

Tate stopped shovelling food into her mouth and swallowed. She took a swig of her wine, "what has he said, exactly?"

Irena shrugged her shoulders, and lifted her wine glass to her mouth, "I don't want to get in between, I love you both."

"Did he tell you how he is trying to manipulate me? To organise my finances. To make me sell my shop and home? That he went to see ELLIE? DID HE TELL YOU THIS?" Tate's voice rose to a shrill.

"Whoa, take a breath, calm it. You just went from 0 to 100 in about a second. What the hell is going on?"

"Mind if I smoke?" Tate stood up and grabbed her bag from the banister.

"If you stand by the balcony, it's not so bad, but you know I would rather you didn't." Irena opened a large blue cupboard and pulled out a glass ashtray, "here, use this."

Tate took the ashtray and placed it on the shelf next to the balcony, "and to top off my fucking day, I bought fags. And now I am smoking them. I'm so angry."

"Well, if that's what you need today, then do it." Irena was busy lighting incense and candles around the room. "I think we have some work to do with your stress levels, when did you last come to one of my classes?"

"Ages ago," Tate blew her smoke out of the door, but it came straight back in, "For fucks sake." She stubbed out the cigarette with force, it split, and tobacco spilled out.

"Here, eat some more, maybe this is because you are hungry," Irena spooned more food onto her plate and then guided her gently into the chair.

Tate picked up her fork and slowly began to eat, "So, what did he tell you?"

"I don't know how to answer you, because I don't want to trigger your anger. So, for tonight, eat and simply be here in the moment with me. Yes?"

Tate nodded and ate until her tummy was full. "What about you? Tell me about you? It always seems to be about me."

"Me? Well, the usual, nothing out of the ordinary. I keep on breathing through the pain and thanking my lucky stars for the good things. You know me..."

"I wish I was you."

"You are exhausted. Maybe you are coming down with something?" Irena pushed her palm across Tate's forehead, "A little hot, but then you are all fired up. You need a rest, let me get you a blanket, and you can snuggle on the sofa whilst I clear up. Here, take your wine."

Tate slumped down into the plush sofa and curled up in a ball, her weary eyes grew heavy, and slumber carried her away.

ELLIE

Living at the villa and having less to do, surprisingly, made Ellie feel more relaxed, despite who she remained a guest of. Making full use of his pool and hot tub, was her priority. Sometimes under the watchful eye of Tony, who would wave or stand still like stone, but at other times she was alone. It was then she pretended to be staying with some gorgeous, rich bloke, and having the time of her life. She kept reminding herself, it could be a lot worse, for now it was relatively calm.

The food was delicious. Tony employed his own personal chef, who happily catered to his every whim. She was loving it and had a similar taste in food to Tony. It beat her diet of fags, coke and the occasional tapas. Somewhere in the depths of her mind, she knew this would all end, that he would demand something of her, likely something big too. But she chose to shelf this nagging thought and enjoy the moment.

The twins were gone, but they were no loss as they ignored her attempt at conversation anyway. Only thing she discovered was that they weren't twins but looked insanely alike. Weird. Maybe they had some sort of cosmetic surgery? As she sat in the hot tub, Tony brought out a flute of chilled champagne, "Here, we are celebrating."

"Oh? Thanks," she took the glass and sipped, it was pink – her favourite.

"So, when you're done, come inside and we can go over some paperwork."

"Paperwork? Is this to do with my money?" Ellie could not suppress her smile.

"Maybe, you'll see." Tony turned and Ellie watched him disappear around the corner. It was nearly the end of it all...finally. Tears pricked her eyes, and she realised how relieved she felt. Downing the remaining fizz, she climbed out of the water and wrapped her oversized fluffy towel around her body. Before she pushed through the door, she towel-dried away any drips, to ensure she would not mark the floor inside. Pissing Tony off was not on her agenda.

"That was quick," Tony sat around the corner past the bar, smoke plumed from his fat Cuban cigar, "here, sit."

She padded around, firmly tucked her towel in, so it covered her bikini, and perched on the edge of the wicker chair, opposite. A round table sat between them.

"These are contracts, law binding. They will ensure you are given possession of the florist and the house which belongs to Tate."

"What?" Ellies eyes widened, "How did you get her to sign them over?"

"Hmmm, well I was getting to that part. We need to get her here, then I can use some gentle persuasion."

Ellie slumped and her mouth curled down. It wasn't over, but at least it explained why he needed her to move in for a while, and it was for her benefit after all. "How are we going to get her here? She will never come," she shook her head and droplets of water settled on the paperwork.

Tony stared, "Watch what you're doing, I told you these are legal documents." He turned the paperwork face down. "Don't be so sure, I had one of my girls draft a little letter, let's just say, it will gnaw away at her, she will come. She will come, to save you."

"Me? She hates me, she won't risk coming here, for ME! It's a flawed plan," Ellie flinched as soon as the words left her mouth. So much for keeping quiet and playing the game.

Tony sprang to his feet. His towering stature loomed above her, casting a shadow across her face, "What the fuck do you know? You better hope she does come for you...No one else will."

"Sorry, I'm sorry," Ellie put her hands up in defeat and lowered her head. "You know what my mouth is like, it's a great plan, really. What I meant was, why would she want to save me?"

Tony sat back down, breathing heavily, "Because I know her, she won't want you on her conscience. She will come. You'll see."

"Will she tell me what happened to my dad too, do you think?"

Tony nodded, "All you need to do, is leave it to me."

"Shall I sign them then?"

Tony laughed, "Don't be stupid, we need her here first, so for now, sit tight and behave, okay? You'll have it all soon enough, she won't hang about once she reads the letter, she will hate the thought that you could be here with me."

"So, can I go back into the hot tub...and maybe a top up?" Ellie wondered if she was pushing her luck.

Tony glared and with a forced smile he answered, "Sure, help yourself, I'll have the girls set up an ice bucket right next to the tub."

Ellie twirled and swiftly marched away before he could change his mind. Perhaps she could finally get everything owed to her...If Tate took the bait and came to 'save her', Tony would ensure she signed the documents. In the meantime, if she could only think before speaking, this life wasn't so bad...

"Oh, and Ellie," Tony called. Ellie turned on her heels, Tony's head stuck out of the door, "I've noticed a little tension between you and my driver."

"What do you mean? He hates me, yes because I hurt him."

Tony shook his head, "On the contrary, I think you'll find it's all sexual tension."

Ellie shivered. "I really think he hates me."

"Not at all, in fact, in about half an hour, he will be coming here for a drink with you, right in here, on this very sofa. This is a holiday after all, what happens in Spain, stays in Spain..." he winked.

What was this? Ellies stomach lurched. She wasn't going to get away so easily after all. He was good looking and similar in age to her, well more so than Tony. But unease refused to leave her as she recalled all their encounters. Not once had he given her the impression of anything but disgust.

"Okay? Half an hour, and don't worry, I won't be watching you, I already told you – you aren't my type at all," Tony called.

"Yes," her voice cracked. "Yes Tony, great." She climbed into the hot tub. She would need to keep playing this game, whatever the game was. It seemed to change all the time and there appeared to be no rules, except that she needed to do as she was told. Maybe she could enjoy some meaningless sex, and it would all be fine. But the goose-bumps which now covered her body, despite the warmth of the water, told her otherwise.

TATE

Tate ran straight into the office pushing away hazy memories, buried in the back of her mind, of when she last visited. The floor to ceiling two-way mirror was still in place, she shuddered at the thought. Behind it in the 'observing' room, her feet automatically sped to the drawer of the desk. The key to the door, where she suspected Ellie would be held, was always kept there before, during her own time there. She crossed her fingers and pushed papers around, feeling up inside, "Thank God," she silently whispered, as she unhooked it from where it dangled. Relief washed over her, and she gave a tiny nod to the old Tate, for enduring everything they put her through back in the day, which meant she was able to navigate quickly around.

Her journey to the house, had been full of nervous energy, and she was barely in control of the car as her legs shook violently. A vow, to never return, was about to be broken, and she prayed this wasn't a doomed mission. What choice did she have? She must help Ellie. Around the back of Tony's swept a barely used road, peppered with utility-style buildings. To the untrained eye, they appeared as though they belonged to the local authority, but they were used for other purposes, when 'big things' were going down. The rest of the time, they were empty, and she hoped this was still the case, otherwise she wouldn't even make it through the first hurdle. So far, so good.

Her car stood completely hidden from view, behind a garage, and she scanned the area to reassure herself that the cameras still looked inward. Tony had often joked, that he didn't care what was going on outside, because NO ONE could enter his land without being spotted, and once they did, they would never leave unless he allowed it. Adrenaline shot through her, she was about to test his theory, with her inside knowledge. "Fuck you Tony," she mouthed.

There was only one camera she was concerned with, and she remembered a blind spot directly beneath it, which she could take advantage of. She hoped to be in and out within minutes. If it took any longer, or if she stumbled into the path of anyone, it was game over. It was a suicide mission really, but it was too late to back out.

With the key in hand, she darted from the windowless room, around to the left and into a short corridor, counting the doors, until she reached the second from the end, where she turned the key and flung open the door.

"Oh my God Ellie...are you ok?"

Ellie crouched in the dark corner, as if she was trying to disappear into the shadows, "Come on, we need to leave now."

Ellie nodded and grabbed her hands, but her moves were slow and deliberate, "Move now, we have to go."

The door closed behind her, and Tate spun to face Tony. It was too late. They were trapped.

"Well, what have we got here? I suppose you couldn't keep away, eh? This place too much of a draw to you?" Tony grabbed her bottom hard and pulled her in tight to him, "Hmm, always did have a firm tight arse, Tate..."

Tate swiped away his hands, and he grabbed her wrist and twisted her arm up behind her back, "did you really think you could get in here, without being spotted? I've been expecting you and even you aren't stupid enough to try coming in the front gates." He laughed and shook his head, "Still so predictable. Right, onwards, this way ladies."

Ellie followed and Tony pushed them both onto the sprawling sofa, "Sit. Please, sit."

Tate felt sick and her wrist throbbed. He brought across two drinks, and handed them one each, "Cannot have my guests going thirsty now."

"Don't drink it Ellie," Tate instructed and knocked her drink to the floor.

Ellie looked to Tony who gave a nod, and she swiped a hefty blow to Tate's cheek. Tate tasted blood in her mouth and her head reeled with the impact.

"Who put you in charge?" Ellie laughed.

Tony chuckled his way to the door and closed it behind him, observing them both. He stood silent. Tate realised in the moment of quiet that Ellie was part of Tony's plan, and they had both lured her there. But why? Maybe the letter from Jose had something to do with it. Maybe Tony knew where Bill was. If Bill was alive, he would kill her. But why would Bill have waited all this time, and why had Tony? Was this their combined revenge on her? Tate's breathing sped with every fresh thought.

"Now, both of you are familiar with this space, of course you are! But not for the same reasons." Tony seemed to relish playing this 'role', narrator to an imaginary audience. "Tate many a night you lay on your back, right here in fact. And you Ellie, you with your broken moral compass, would have gladly given me everything should I have wanted it...oh and how was your brief encounter with my driver? I take it you fulfilled his every whim?"

Tate looked towards Ellie, who it seemed had not escaped unscathed from this sorry situation. Now, with the light from the window, her face was a little puffy and her eye slightly blackened, but she said nothing, briefly looking away and then fixing her eyes, defiantly on Tony.

"I didn't choose this Tony, you trapped and abused me. You kidnapped me, and trafficked me, like some commodity – what choice did I have?" Tate spat her words towards him with venom.

"Did I say your moral compass was broken? No, I didn't. Not like this one," he smiled. "But, the money, shall we discuss this now? I always find talking about money so vulgar, don't you? But let's be honest here Tate, you were happy enough to set up a new life for yourself with money from my world. Let's all sit with that for a moment, shall we, Saint Tate?"

Tate's cheeks flushed. Those words echoed Leo, he wasn't being 'judgy' or controlling after all. He was right, that part of her life could never be fully over whilst she built her life out of their money. Why did it always take something so drastic for her to see clearly?

"Now I have both of your attention, I would like to begin my big reveal." He clapped his hands and one of his girls wheeled through an elderly man, covered in a blanket with a bald head. His eyes cast down towards his knees. Tony smiled as both Tate and Ellie sat still, wondering what this big reveal meant. Tate sighed in relief, that it wasn't Bill he brought out, and looked to Ellie, who appeared bewildered. She was clearly not in on this part either.

The girl parked the wheelchair next to the large mirror. The man lifted his head and looked towards Ellie and then Tate. Tears sprung from his eyes.

"Still nothing?" Tony clapped his hands with glee and revelled in the moment.

"What are we meant to do? What is this?" Ellie enquired pointing towards the newest arrival to their circus.

Tate studied the old man as Tony whipped the blanket from his lap. His fused hands sat motionless on his thighs. The wrinkles on his face were scarring, the bald head, also lined and damaged. He wasn't old necessarily, he was *burned*. She looked back into his eyes, and shivered, those eyes...

"What the fuck have you done Tony?" Tate screamed and held her hand over her mouth.

"Ah," Tony shook his arms in a cheer, "it seems we have a clear winner; the game is finally up Bill. Ellie, may I present to you, your dear old dad."

Ellie stood slowly and walked towards the wheelchair. Her eyes fixed on his, which pleaded with sadness and fear. "This is my dad?" She pointed accusingly at him, and Bill nodded in return.

Tony pushed in close, "Sorry love, but daddy can't speak," he made a sad face and put on a fake forlorn voice, "he lost it in the fire, and most of his mobility and skin."

"You mean you rescued him?" Ellie looked to Tony and then to Bill.

"Well rescue is a strong term, and I am not sure he feels rescued, do ya Bill? But yes, he owes me his life."

Ellie's anger erupted, "You had him here all this time, and never once told me?" Her clenched fist caught Tony in his stomach, and he doubled over. Bill jolted and silently screamed.

Tate jumped to Ellie's defence and caught the blow meant for her. She fell to the floor, "she's only a kid Tony."

"Not much younger than you were Saint Tate, old enough to know better."

Tate gingerly stood up and rubbed her chin as her tongue checked her teeth for damage.

"I've been brought here, terrorised and ordered around for, *this*, to be shown," she flicked her head towards Bill. "What am I supposed to do with it? I can't give him a good send off, a memorial and I'm not being fucking saddled with him."

Tate gasped, "You selfish bitch. To think I worried about you, in fact I am here because of you. And all you care about is yourself."

Tony lit a cigarette, "Well, Bill, this is going even better than I planned," He exhaled his smoke into Bill's face. "Didn't I tell you Ellie, the first time we met out there in my garden, how like your dad you are. Ruthless. Selfish. It's not easy always being right. Bill you must be proud."

"You always were a bully, now you've stooped to the utterly defenceless." Tate's anger rose and she refused to flinch when Tony slapped her face. Adrenaline kicked in. She knew there was no way out of this, and she would not go down without some sort of fight.

"My best revenge tactic ever. He has watched every interaction played out here between Ellie and me. We even recorded it all, in case he missed it live. That way he is reminded how vulnerable his little girl is. Watching just how far she was willing to go, for money and drugs. It felt amazing to be fair. Least effort on my part too. I mean it's cost me, don't get me wrong, cost me a lot financially. Doctors, surgeons, medications and their utter discretion too. But the best bit, before today, was watching him squirm, when those women who used to throw themselves at him, now dressed his wounds and pitied him. Chatted in his ear shot about what a relief it was they weren't involved with him. Mr vain himself taken apart and unrecognisable."

Tony recounted his monologue like a poet, with a soft voice and like a cherished collection of memories. Bill stared towards Ellie, but her face offered no comfort. "I think the thing that may have just finally finished him off, in fact, I thought he was going to faint at the time, was when you," he patted Ellie's head, "his little girl, got ruffed up, and let's just say a bit more than you bargained for, by my driver..." Tony glared at Bill. "You wished you died in that fire, huh Bill. But we get along, don't we?" Tony sat on the arm of the chair next to Bill and squeezed his shoulder in mock affection.

Bill sat as still as stone.

"You've finally lost your shit Tony," Tate spoke quietly.

"Shut up," Ellie began by speaking, but her voice rose into a shrill, which echoed around the room. "JUST SHUT THE FUCK UP! You," she pointed to Tony, "said you would help me get my money back and find out what happened to my dad, but all along, you had him creepily watching me...That's fucking sick. YOU ARE A SICK FUCK OLD MAN!"

Tony's movement was quicker than lightening, and he grabbed Ellie by her throat and smashed her against the wall next to Bill. "Less of the old man, please." He shook his head and tutted, "The youth of today." He held her for a moment and threw her to the ground in front of her father.

"Now beg me for help."

But Ellie stood, straightened herself up and stared at Tony. She was undeniably fierce, or naïve and reckless. Maybe a mixture of them all, but Tate gasped for her safety.

"I. Said. Beg." Tony's face was twisted but his words calm.

Ellie stood firm but Tate's heart felt as though it would beat out of her chest. Ellie couldn't possibly know what Tony was capable of, she hadn't seen the brutality that Tate had witnessed. "Tony, please leave her."

"I don't need your help," Ellie spoke but her eyes remained firmly locked with Tony's. Tony would be enjoying this inter-lude, it would be fun for him, and Ellie was still clueless.

"I told her to beg, not you, Saint Tate. After everything she has done to you, and still you stay on this doomed mission to save this...brat...I would be more concerned with my own safety if I were you." Tony's irritation increased and his face twitched.

"You don't know what the fuck you're doing, Ellie," Tate shouted, ignoring Tony, as helpless tears streamed down Bill's face.

Tony turned and marched to the door at the back of the room. He returned with a worn tatty briefcase. Bill's eyes widened and Tate shuddered. She knew what the contents of this bag were and fought the urge to run. Where could she run to? She couldn't get out of this one. This was it, her and Bill's worlds really were inextricably tied right up until the end. She stared at what Bill had   become and felt nothing, except maybe a tinge of pity. The once strong, delicious man was now helpless and completely at the mercy of Tony. His worst nightmare a reality, and now to watch his daughter being ruthlessly played like a cat with a defenceless, clueless mouse. He was unable to protect her, and instead forced to watch.

Ellie had tricked Tate into coming to her rescue, but she re-fused to believe that she had any idea about the ramifications her actions would cause. Now, as she watched her reactions unfold towards her own father, she understood that Ellie was not like other people and that maybe this world was as much hers as Bill's.

Tony was busy methodically laying out his tools along the bar. Ellies eyes widened, and reality seemed to dawn on her: torture. She threw herself at his feet and clung to his calves, "Please, please don't kill me." Tony kicked her away and she crawled straight back, "I'm on your side, you know I would do anything for you, whatever you need." Tony ignored her pathetic pleas an continued to arrange his apparatus.

He turned to his captive audience, "Ladies and gentlemen," his outstretched arms as though welcoming an invisible crowd to his circus. "Roll up! Roll up! Today we have an ensemble not to be missed. We have father, daughter and whore!" He pointed to each of them in turn.

Tate thought she would wet herself, and fear gripped her legs. She slumped to the chair and shook. Tony really had cracked this time. He had finally gone mad. Why did she think that she could single- handedly, save Ellie? She ignored all the warnings from everyone who loved her, to leave it alone. Even Celia told her to say clear. Now the danger was imminent, and it was all too late for her.

"We have a truly memorable act today, and I present first – the daughter." He yanked Ellie up by her hair until she stood beside him. Her face paled as she glanced at the neat line of tools. Still no tears but her lips narrowed and her breath heavy. "Tony, kill them first. Please, I will help you." She whispered, but it was loud enough for both Bill and Tate to hear.

"Stop ruining my show. I told you, you are way too vocal, you need to work on that." Tony spoke as though telling off a young child. Tate gasped at Ellie's offer and realised that she was beyond any help.

"I have to tell you, that the impact of what you are about to see, may be less powerful than planned, as I imagined forcing a devoted daughter's hand. It seems that the daughter we have here, loves her money more than her daddy. Poor Bill. But hey ho, we can make it work. I mean, I had no idea baby girl would show up, I was happy enough enjoying your pitiful existence. Imagine, I don't think you can, but try..." Tony emulated a Shakespearean actor with his performance, "to imagine how stoked I was when she arrived in Spain. It was an opportunity I could not miss." Tony gripped Ellie's chin between his finger and thumb and her face twisted in pain, "In fact, if you hadn't headed up this way, I would have enticed you here with your love of the white stuff...boy does she love that powder Billy boy!"

Tate turned to Bill, his eyes, fixed on Ellie, expressed anger and frustration and she knew how much this situation would be eating away at him.

Tony pushed Ellie away, "It couldn't have worked out better... got to even up an old score, with our friend Saint Tate here," he smiled and bowed his head in pretend admiration. "She never bothered me enough to waste resources on before, but I'm not one to ignore a decent chance at settling old scores, and you were practically served up on a plate...perfect way to hook our little money grabber Ellie here..."

"I'm sure we all appreciate you clarifying the current situation, especially with such feeling," Tate scowled. "So, you're going to kill us all now, how original."

Tony ignored Tate and continued, "Today, will be the final curtain, for our poor old friend Bill. He would probably beg for the end, on a normal day, if he had a voice. But at the hands of his daughter? Hmm, not so sure. What do you say Bill?" Tony bent until his nose almost touched Bill's and spoke slowly and deliberately, as though Bill could not understand, "WHAT. DO. YOU. SAY. BILL?"

Tate knew Bill understood everything that was being said and done, and he would make it easy on Ellie. Tate looked towards her, expecting to see a quivering mess, but her faced conveyed relief, and it seemed she believed she would be ok.

"Ellie don't do it. He'll kill you next, he's going to kill us all…"

Tony grabbed something shiny from the table and swiped towards Tate. She blacked out with the impact of a fierce blow to her head.

ELLIE

A pool of blood, congealed beside Tate's lifeless head. Her hair splayed out like a discarded wig on the floor. Tony had lost his mind. All the promises of a big reveal were true, her unrecognisable dad sat with fear in his eyes, across the room. He was alive, he was here. But it was all merely a game. Tony didn't want to help her, and all those tasks he asked her to do in return, well they were just for fun – they served no purpose. He didn't give a toss about Tate, not enough to bother revenging her up until Ellie's arrival. No, Tate was only the carrot, to fire her up, to focus her attention whilst Tony played out his revenge on her dad. What a stupid girl. So much for knowing what she was doing and being in control, on reflection she couldn't remember the last time she was in control, if ever.

It was a lot to take in. No one was looking for her, or her dad. They could easily disappear, her dad was already 'dead' and she, well it would be months before anyone looked for her. That was her own fault, her mum was beginning to accept that she didn't bother to contact her and was messaging less and less. Her legs wobbled as Tony circled Bill, tapping pliers in the palm of his hand and bile crept up her throat. Tears flooded her eyes, snot dripped from her nose, and she realised she was crying. Her chest heaved and wails escaped her mouth, "Please don't hurt me, haven't I done what you told me? I can carry on, I could be one of your girls, I promise I've learned my lesson."

Tony stopped next to her and stared. A chill shook her body.

"You're a mess, I can barely understand you through your sobs," he spoke in a calm voice, as though discussing the weather or what to have for tea, "but it looks like I may have finally broken you. I mean, it was tough, you are tough. Chip off the old block eh Bill?" He smiled, "But you, Ellie, are a selfish young woman. I haven't seen a single trait worth saving. You didn't even care when I brought your poor old man in," He shook his head, "and he could make the toughest weep in sympathy, I mean, look at him!" Tony turned towards Bill and wiped away an invisible tear. "You poor guy. Nothing left of you really, is there? Oh, apart from her, she is very much alive and kicking for now, and you could say she is part of you. I feel a change of plan coming on…"

Ellie wiped her eyes and nose with her vest and sniffed hard. From the corner of her eye, she noticed Tate's mobile in the back pocket of her shorts. If she could get close enough, she could call for help, that seemed her only chance. Inching to her knees, she examined Tate's head carefully as her fingers gently rubbed her scalp and neck. Tony spun around, "Sudden concern from the brat? What is she up to?" He held his chin between his fingers and looked up to ceiling as though in deep thought. "Let me see…."

Ellie's hand rested on Tate's back, as though she was checking for breath. She was so close, one little movement more, and she would grab the phone…

Her shriek pierced the room, as Tony's foot crushed her hand. The crack of her finger bones induced vomit and she threw up down her front. He reached down into Tate's pocket and removed the phone, keeping pressure on her shattered hand. Tate still did not move, despite his force. Perhaps she was dead. Tears streamed from Ellie's eyes and her face paled as Tony lifted his leg and kicked Ellie away from Tate in one powerful swipe. She crashed to the floor and writhed in pain, "Help! Please help me!" she yelled.

"Oh, there's no one here that will help you…you know that. Even your old man is helpless." He tossed the phone to the floor and smashed it with the heel of his foot.

"Now. Where was I?" he tapped the pliers onto his palm, and then returned them to the bar top. "Oh yes, my change of plan, Bill, let's rid the world of this nasty piece of work, then I will decide whether to keep you for a bit longer, you know to let the enormity of today sink in..." Tony smiled. "First, let's get you ready Ellie." He swung his head until it was inches away and whispered, "Take off your clothes."

Ellie shook her head, "No, I won't," tears muffled her words.

"I'm sorry, but I thought you dared say no to me," Tony yanked her hair back and with the other hand ripped off her vest. "You really should wear a bra young lady, it's not ladylike to walk around without one." He pinched her nipples and Bill's silent sobs choked him. "Now, in case my hearing is playing up, I will ask you again. Take of your clothes."

"Get off me, you fucking animal," Ellie spat in Tony's face, and kicked and screamed as adrenaline coursed through her. He wiped his face and glared; his eyes bore into her flesh like a laser beam, and his first punch to her stomach, winded her. She collapsed to the floor clutching her knees to her chest and he kicked her hard in the back.

"You've learned nothing, nothing. It's disappointing, Ellie," he spoke whilst choosing a tool, and his fingers rested on a screwdriver.

Ellie shrieked. Bill closed his eyes tight. This was the end.

Tony loomed above her, and she held her breath. Suddenly a piercing alarm sounded, and her hands flew to her ears. Tony stopped still and looked around. He ran behind the two-way mirror into the viewing room and picked up a phone, "Understood. Execute evacuation."

He lingered in the doorway for a moment, as though weighing up his next move and launched himself at Bill's wheelchair. Bill's head cracked on the tiled floor. Ellie grappled with the edge of the sofa, her head spun, and her legs shook as Tony held her down with all his weight and gripped tightly around her neck, blackness crept across her vision, as she struggled for breath, until darkness enveloped her.

TATE

"Eileen, she's strong, she will come out of this, you'll see," Irena's unmistakeable voice, was the first thing she heard. Her eyes refused to open, and her body felt like stone.

Eileen sobbed.

"Here, use this." Was that Leo's whisper? Where *was* she? She tried to pull apart her eyelids, they moved but shut tight immediately.

"Did you see that?"

"What?" Irena's voice sounded closer.

"Her eyes, they opened for like a second, it was only a second but they definitely moved." She could feel Leo's breath on her face, and his scent of Armani aftershave, awoke something within her, like a dose of smelling salts.

She pulled up her lids again, this time they stayed open, but her vision was blurry, and she could see only shadowy movement.

"Tate! Darling!" Her mum's voice kissed her ears, and salty tears streamed from her eyes.

"Get a doctor, quick, she's awake!" Irena yelled, her voice croaky and broken.

She stared at one figure, and allowed her eyes to adjust, like the lens of a camera preparing to focus on an object. After a few moments, her room filled with medics who swiftly completed observations, and various beeping machines silenced, her blurriness cleared.

"You can see me, can't you?" Her mum squeezed her hand and lifted it up to her lips, kissing it over and over. Tate nodded and her lips curled slightly upwards.

Irena sat at her feet; mascara smeared eyes streamed, but her mouth pursed in relief. Then there he was, Leo. Stood at the foot of her bed, his expressionless face staring, and his mouth firmly shut. Her hand rubbed her throat, she was parched and so exhausted.

"Get her water Irena, she needs water. Here, my baby girl, take a sip." her mum pushed a straw into her mouth, and she gently sipped, coughed, and rested her head back on the pillow. Sleep crept over her once more.

***

Sitting up in bed, Tate felt the familiar rumblings of her hungry tummy and wondered what lunchtime would bring. Her appetite returning, symbolised the beginnings of recovery and she could not wait to get out of hospital. The staff were amazing, and had taken great care of her, but she felt her recovery would be speedier from home. Her mum was there to look after her, after all. If she could convince the doctor of this fact...

"Hey Chica!" Behind a huge bouquet of flowers, jingled the unmistakable sound of Irena, "I know you aren't allowed these in here, but let's see if we can get away with it eh?"

She plonked them down on the little cupboard next to Tate's bed, and leaned in for a careful hug, "You definitely look better today."

"I am, I can't wait to get out of here now!"

"Hey, steady! You cannot rush this..."

"I know..."

"Listen, I'm not going to waste my breath telling you how angry I was, that you thought you could go to Tony's alone and not even tell anyone...because I told you this, enough times when you were unconscious, I'm so glad you are back with us!"

"Phew, I hate being in your bad books," Tate patted the bed, "Sit."

"But my nerves are shot, and you have to promise NEVER to ever do anything like that again? Will you?"

Tate nodded, silent guilt ate away at her, "I'm so sorry for everything I put you through."

"You know they haven't caught him?"

"Tony? No surprise there, once someone has that much power, people blindly follow instructions...I've seen it with my own eyes. Can't believe he will come back around here though; he'll lay low for a while someplace else."

"You're not even scared? That he may come back for you?"

"It wasn't me he was after, I was only being used, as part of revenge on Bill, in his big plan."

"Bill. Can't believe he was still alive."

"Alive but not living, existing," Tate shuddered, "It was like living in hell for him I should think. Leo is right, karma is a bitch. When is the funeral?"

"Next week, can't imagine they'll be many in the mourning party, Ellie was flown home for burial close to her mum."

"She couldn't be saved you know. I tried, but she only cared about herself. She would have done anything to me, to save her own skin. Offered to help Tony..." Tate's breathing sped and she wiped her eyes with her dressing gown sleeve.

"Too much like her old man for her own good, you couldn't have done any more than you did."

Tate nodded, "I know that."

"You know, Leo has been beside himself, it was him that called the authorities. He saw on your snapchat, where you were, and sent the Police, to look for a kidnapped local."

"Local?" Tate scratched her head.

"Had to be economical with the truth to pique their interest. Did the trick in the nick of time, for you at least."

"He hasn't been back since I woke up, he's probably had enough. He hates drama."

"Sure, he hates drama, and let's face it, he's had a lot of that since he got involved with you. But I think you'll find, he's staying away because he thinks you aren't interested. The last time you spoke to him, was at his office."

"He threw me out," Tate fired back.

"Hmm, I'm not entirely sure how accurate your account is, and anyway, he barely left your side before you woke." Irena stood up and rummaged in her patchwork bag, "Here."

Tate took the mobile phone and smiled.

"I have programmed in our numbers for you, now you can message us whilst you are in here recovering."

Sobs erupted and Tate's fragile body shook. Her mind whirled. Irena was always mopping up her messes, smoothing things out for her, and rarely asked for anything in return. Why? What sort of a friend was she to Irena? Crap. Selfish and crap.

"Here, wipe your nose, you've got a snot bubble," Irena passed the tissues to Tate. "You know how I hate snot."

Tate smiled through her tears, and wiped her face, "I need to be a better friend to you. Everything you have done and still do for me...I can never thank you enough."

"This 'incident' is making you mushy, but now I come to think of it, you are right, you do need to be a better friend..." Irena stuck out her tongue and then hugged Tate. "You have some making up to do...not just with me either. If you look on that mobile, the numbers you need right now, are on there. So, no excuses, I cannot have Leo keep harassing me about how you are." She pecked a kiss on Tate's cheek. "I have to go now, Jo is looking after both shops, and I promised to be an hour at most."

"God, how is Jo? I haven't even asked."

"Jo is great. Passed her final exam and is keen for you to get better so we can all celebrate together. Her number is also in your phone, so you can send her a 'well done' message."

"Amazing news, maybe things are looking up already. You think of everything."

"Love you, Adios." She swept out of the door in a jingle of bangles and the waft of lilies tickled Tate's nose. She smiled and leant back on her pillow, with a yawn.

A little later, Tate typed and deleted a message to Leo. What should she say? How could she begin? She knew, when in the clutches of danger, she realised how wrong she had been. Maybe that was where she should begin. He wasn't trying to control her or take over her life. He genuinely cared and as an outsider, was more equipped to see her situation for what it was. Sadly, this meant that the shop needed to be sold and her home too. Perhaps she could move back with Irena, but her business? And Ellie was dead, she no longer needed the money, so maybe it was all finally over. Leo would not accept that idea, of that, she was sure. But all her money, apart from a tiny profit, was the so called 'dirty money'. Pain seared across her head as her thoughts swirled. There was no immediate answer, and she closed her eyes...

One step at a time, that was what Irena would tell her. Begin with something you *can* do. The only thing was messaging:

CONGRATULATIONS JO! KNEW YOU COULD DO IT. CANNOT WAIT TO CELEBRATE & THANKS SO MUCH FOR HELPING OUT WITH THE SHOP. TATE XX

HEY MUM, DOING OK, CANNOT WAIT TO COME HOME. LOVE YOU. TATE XX

Finally, she crossed her fingers as she pressed 'send' to Leo. Despite what Irena thought, he could easily have decided to call it a day, after everything.

LEO, ITS TATE, NEW NUMBER. JUST HI REALLY. AND THANKS FOR HELPING ME COME BACK, IRENA SAID YOU WERE HERE WITH ME A LOT. HOPE TO SEE YOU SOON. XX

She put down the phone, but it immediately beeped.

TATE! OMG I'M SO GLAD YOU ARE GOING TO BE OK. PLEASE DON'T WORRY – I HAVE THE SHOP COVERED. WILL COME AND SEE YOU WHEN YOU ARE FEELING UP TO IT. JO XX

The second beep: "DARLING, WE WILL HAVE YOU HOME BE-FORE YOU KNOW IT. GET SOME REST AND I WILL VISIT LATER. LOVE YOU XX MUM

No third beep. She checked the message had been delivered, and it showed as 'read'. Tate sighed. What did she expect? That he was sitting around, waiting for her to message? "Grow up Tate," she despised herself sometimes.

The door opened, it was her favourite nurse, "Oh Tate, you cannot have those flowers in here, let me take them for you. Next visitor you have can take them away again. Don't say a word though, I shouldn't do that." Her thick Spanish accent was cheerful and when she smiled, her teeth gleamed.

"Lucia, I want you to have them, take them home with you. If I wasn't stuck in here, I would have brought you them anyway. You do an amazing job. Thank you."

"Aww, thank you. They are beautiful, if you are sure?"

"Yes. Absolutely, well deserved. And when I am better, I will create you a bouquet with my own hands."

Lucia squeezed her arm, and then took her blood pressure, "I'm going to need to do your 'obs', ok? Have to take care of you, especially after our little discovery..."

Tate put her finger to her lips and nodded. Familiar with the routine, she looked towards the window, leading to the corridor. Peeking between the blades of the blind, was a pair of blue eyes and a smattering of freckles. Her heart raced, and her face flushed.

"Someone to see you I think," she winked and lifted the flowers up, inhaling their scent, "I will enjoy these," she held open the door for Leo and headed off towards the nurses' locker room.

Leo stood in front of the visitor's chair, "Is this seat taken?"

Tate beamed, "Yes, I mean, no."

"Shall I stay Tate? Or should I go?"

"Definitely stay, please."

Leo leant down and kissed her gently but firmly on the lips, "Shall we start again? Like we just met in Miguel's? No more drama?"

"You saved my life," Tate gripped his hand and kissed it.

"So, I'm your hero? Is that what you're saying?" Leo's eyes narrowed.

"Don't push your luck," Tate laughed, "But, for today, yes, you are my hero."

Leo perched on the edge of the bed, "I'll take that. I wish I'd known though, because I could have worn my big pants over my trousers..."

"Oh, promise you will show me once I get out of here? That would really make me smile. Anyway, how did you get here so quickly? You were here within ten minutes?"

Leo leaned in closer, "I was sat in my car, deciding whether to come in or give you space, needed a sign, I guess. Then you messaged and in I came." He sighed, "All I want is for you to be mine."

"Do you really mean that?" Tate's stomach fluttered, "when did you first realise?"

"When you blamed your mojito for your verbal diarrhoea, instead of admitting it was because you fancied me."

"They were very strong mojito's," Tate pulled him close, "but you are right, I was instantly attracted to you. Very much and even more so now." She kissed his lips and tears rolled down her cheeks. This was the beginning of a new chapter in her life. Finally, she would leave behind the darkness, the shade. And the miracle baby, clinging to life within her, would be their line, drawn in the sand. But for now, at least, that secret was hers alone.

Tate awoke with the force of something sharp piercing the skin on her arm. Her eyes opened to a man in a white coat, a doctor, she assumed, looking down on her.

"What are you doing? What's happened?" She winced in pain.

"Shh, it's a little something to help you settle, to sleep."

"But I was settled," her words slurred.

"Thrashing about you were, a sedative is what you need."

"Stop, please..." but the effects were already taking control and she felt heavy and weak.

"Message from Tony, give him the money from the shop and house, and he will leave you alone. Call this solicitor, who will draft the documents, you will have to sign, that's all and it's over. For good. I will leave the details in your florist, next to Celia's name card in your contact's box. When you get back to work, get it sorted. Then you can stop looking over your shoulder, especially if you have something so fragile to protect now..." he pointed to her stomach. How could he have known? No one knew except her and the staff...but unable to fight the effects any longer...sleep took her.

***

"Hey, sleepyhead. That was one long rest,"

"How long?"

"Well, its midday now, ready for something to eat? They have said you can come home soon. Final check today that all is well, and then home for more r & r."

Tate smiled, and rubbed her still heavy head as a hazy thought about the florist popped in. It was dreamlike and inaccessible, "Mum, you will stay won't you? I mean I don't want you to go back to the UK yet?"

"Eileen tenderly kissed her head, "Of course, I'm going nowhere until you are up and on your feet. Besides it seems Bella is being spoiled rotten at Auntie Pat's house, so she isn't even missing me."

Tate grabbed her hand, "I need to tell you something, it's a secret though, not a soul knows except for the staff."

Eileen leaned in close and whispered into her ear, "I'm going to be a granny!" Her eyes filled with happy tears, and Tate's brow furrowed in confusion. "I wasn't meant to hear, but I was waiting to come in and see you, and two staff members were discussing you…" she rubbed Tate's hands and kissed them, "I haven't told a soul but how do you feel about it?"

"I have no idea what Leo will feel about it? But, I am getting used to the idea…and feel like it's a huge incentive to get better and back on my feet… I am worried though, that's why I was going to tell you, I mean my body has been through so much since, since I conceived…"

"Well, shall I have a word with the nurse, see if there are any tests you can have? Checks?"

Tate nodded; her voice silenced by overwhelming emotion. Relief washed over her, that she could confide in her mum about it all.

"Okay, let me see what I can find out," Eileen kissed Tate's cheek and swept across the room and out of the door to where the nurse's station sat.

Tate watched through the window as her mum stood in deep conversation with Lucia, her stomach somersaulted, and she gently rubbed it in circle motions, hoping all would be well.

EIGHT MONTHS LATER

Tate pushed up the incline towards Bazaar, with her sleeping baby. The short walk from home, always took three times longer since the arrival of Lily, around every corner was another well-wishing elder willing to shower her with goodwill and love. Tate didn't mind, in fact she revelled in the affection. Leo seemed to have adjusted to fatherhood. After she announced the news, and his ashen face recoloured, they began to plan their next moves and decided to bite the bullet and live together. His once neat house was now strewn with nappies and tiny pink vests. He pretended it was annoying, but she could tell he loved it all being around him. On more than one occasion, she caught him folding Lily's clothing and stacking them into neat piles, whilst he chatted away to his little daughter.

Almost immediately, they had settled into a groove of their own, and it seemed right that they were so quickly at that stage, so early in their relationship. Her mum was in a rental around the corner, desperate not to miss out on any 'firsts' with Lily, and although temporarily living in Spain, Tate was sure she would settle permanently. She was already helping the ladies in Church with the flowers and enjoying weekly yoga classes with Irena.

It seemed like a lifetime ago, since she left that hospital room after the 'Tony' business. So much had happened. On her first day back to work, she was welcomed back by Irena and Jo, with a new apron and coffee and pastries, and the scent of lilies once again tickling her nose. But something had shifted, and she felt unease, but she could not put her finger on it. That first day came and went, uneventfully and all seemed to be normal.

After her first week, she was locking up alone to go home and felt drawn to the contact's box. That was when the clarity returned. Her fingers sifted through the names, and rested on Celia, where a business card with a solicitor's information was pinned. On the back, the handwritten words: Call him and sort it, or forever look over your shoulder.

The card shook in her hand as she recalled the hazy night-visitor in hospital, and the warning he brought with him. Her hand flew to her tummy protectively, and without hesitation, she called the number. The brief exchange of instructions gave little away. She would receive a brown envelope, with the deeds to the shop and house in, which she should sign, have witnessed and then return in the provided envelope. She would have one month to seal up the two shops, so Irena's was once again separate, and clear her things from both properties. Leo was uneasy about the whole thing, but it seemed to be their way out of that world with least interactions. So, he witnessed the documents and walked with her to post it.

Weirdly, it all happened exactly the way she was told. And Leo was right, she felt free and able to look ahead for the first time, if she was honest.

The door to Irena's was open, and soft meditation music wafted out together with the scent of incense. "Look who has come to see you..."

"My Lily! Come in Chica, let me push the pram out the back, here give her to me..." Irena lifted Lily out and peppered kisses all over her head and face, before slumping into the armchair, which was Tate and Lily's favourite catching up spot. The price tag had been removed and it was officially a part of the shop furniture now.

"How are things going with your new neighbour then?" Tate enquired, surprised at how little she felt about it.

"The new sign is up, but I haven't seen many going in yet, not sure how well a beauty shop will do up here, but who knows what it's really about in there, I guess we will have to wait and see." Irena answered but continued to shower Lily with kisses, "Oh, you have grown so much, and in only one day little madam."

Tate sidled outside and lent back on the railing. The front of her old shop was now cream, and the doors and shutters an olive green, it looked pretty with the new window boxes full of greenery. Her eyes focussed in on the window where a figure sat chatting over a counter to a young girl. She nodded and they locked eyes for a moment, and Tate stifled her urge to wave. It was better to leave things distant.

The new sign above the shop, looked chic and simply said, "CELIA'S".

I am thankful to everyone who continues to encourage me with my writing.

My writing really does help me through the dark days of my ME struggles, and if I produce something I can share, and people may enjoy, then that's a win for me.

I plan to continue working on my shorter length stories, and to experiment further with the 'one story, two perspective' element.

Watch out for more stories in the coming year!

This is a complete work of fiction, including characters and scenarios.

Printed in Great Britain
by Amazon